HACKBERRY HOLLAND NOVELS

House of the Rising Sun
Wayfaring Stranger
Feast Day of Fools
Rain Gods
Lay Down My Sword and Shield

BILLY BOB HOLLAND NOVELS

In the Moon of Red Ponies
Bitterroot
Heartwood
Cimarron Rose

OTHER FICTION

The Jealous Kind
Jesus Out to Sea
White Doves at Morning
The Lost Get-Back Boogie
The Convict and Other Stories
Two for Texas
To the Bright and Shining Sun
Half of Paradise

ANOTHER
KIND OF EDEN

ANOTHER KIND OF EDEN

JAMES LEE BURKE

ORION

An Orion paperback
First published in Great Britain in 2021 by Orion Fiction,
an imprint of The Orion Publishing Group Ltd.,
Carmelite House, 50 Victoria Embankment
London EC4Y 0DZ

An Hachette UK Company

1 3 5 7 9 10 8 6 4 2

A CIP catalogue record for this book is
available from the British Library.

ISBN (Mass Market Paperback) 978 1 3987 0471 8
ISBN (eBook) 978 1 3987 0472 5

Printed and bound in Great Britain by Clays Ltd, Elcograf S.p.A.

www.orionbooks.co.uk

In memory of Murphy Dowouis

Prologue

THE EVENTS I'M about to describe may challenge credulity. I do not blame the reader. Young Goodman Brown wanders these pages. The macabre images, the Gothic characters, the perfume from a poisonous garden could have been created with the ink from Nathaniel Hawthorne's pen.

But the operative word is "could." Edwin Arlington Robinson once wrote that God slays Himself with every leaf that flies. I think the same is true of us. I think we cannot understand ourselves until we understand that living is a form of dying. My generation was born during the Great Depression and, for good or bad, will probably be the last generation to remember traditional America. Our deaths may be inconsequential; the fling we had was not.

Cursed or blessed with the two faces of Janus, we saw the past and the future simultaneously but were sojourners in both, and most of us had gone into the night even before we knew the sun had set. In our ephemerality, we were both vain and innocent, as children can be vain and innocent. In our confidence that the evil of German fascism and Japanese imperialism lay smoldering in the ashes of Berlin and Hiroshima, we believed the republic of Jefferson and Adams had become the model for the rest of humankind, without acknowledging the internecine nature of triumphalism.

Music was everywhere. Dixieland, Brubeck, R&B, swing, C&W, rock and roll, Bird. The amusement piers along the Gulf Coast rang with it. In the hurricane season, when the nights were as black as silk, the waves seemed to swallow the stars and turn the waves to burgundy. They were five feet high, hissing with foam, swollen with seaweed and shellfish, with the thudding density of lead, smelling of birth and organic turmoil and destruction; then, suddenly, they would lift you into the air, pinioning your arms behind you like Jesus on his cross, and release you on the sand as a mother would a child.

It was a grand time to be around. War was an aberration. Bergen-Belsen and Changi Prison were devised by foreign lunatics who wore the uniforms of clowns. A GI with a cigarette lighter that had a sketch on the side of Mount Fuji was a celebrity. But the fondest memories were the drive-in theaters, the formal dances under a silver ball, the summer tuxes and hooped crinoline dresses, the dollar-fifty corsages and small boxes of chocolate-covered cherries we gave to our dates at their front door, the flush in a girl's face when you kissed her cheek, the shared conviction that spring was forever and none of us would ever die.

But illusion is illusion, and the millions of bison and passenger pigeons slaughtered on the plains and the whalebones that still wash ashore on the New England coast are testimony to our anthropogenic relationship with the earth. And for that reason I have written this account of the events to which I was witness in the year 1962, in the days just before the Cuban Missile Crisis.

These events fill me with sorrow and give me no peace. They also make me question my sanity. But they occurred, and others can reckon with them or not. I said Goodman Brown found his way into this story. That's not quite accurate. I believe the human story is collective, that we write it together, but only a few are willing to recognize their participation in it. T. E. Lawrence described the aftermath of the Turks at work in an Arabian village. I have never forgotten the images, and I have never forgiven him for implanting them in my memory. At the conclusion of this story, I hope I have not done that to you.

Chapter One

MANY YEARS AGO, knocking around the American West was quite a gig. Think of running alongside a boxcar, your heart bursting in your chest, slinging your duffel and your guitar inside and jumping in after them, and then two hours later descending the Grand Divide, your head dizzy from the thin air, grizzly bears loping alongside the grain cars. The side-door Pullman didn't cost a cent, and what a show it was: an orange moon above a Kansas wheat field; the iridescent spray of wheel lines; the roar of a stream at the bottom of a canyon; the squeak of an irrigation valve at sunset; the cold smell of water seeping through a walnut orchard at evening tide.

Colorado had strange laws back then. Hitchhiking or hopping a freight could cost you six months in the can or on the hard road. The consequence was that bums and migrants riding a hotshot into Denver could get into the state but not out, so Larimer Street was overflowing with panhandlers and derelicts pissing and sleeping in alleyways and under the bridges on the Platte. In the spring of '62, I swung off a flat-wheeler at the Denver city limits and slept two nights in the Sally, then took a Greyhound bus down to Trinidad and hired on with a big dairy and produce farm that provided cabins and community showers and a dining hall for the workers. The owner was Mr. Jude Lowry.

Know why migrants are migrants? There's no yesterday and no tomorrow. Anonymity is a given; migrants come with the dust and go with the wind. Mortality disappears with a cold bottle of beer in a juke joint. I had nonalcoholic blackouts back then, and because of the life I had chosen, I didn't mind. In fact, the migrant way of life seemed created especially for people like me.

Late in August, Mr. Lowry put me in charge of the flatbed and the trailer it towed, and told me to round up Spud Caudill and Cotton Williams and start hauling our last crop of tomatoes down to the packing house in Trinidad, which would take us three trips. The air was heavy with the odor of insecticide and the harrows busting up the soil and the scattered chunks of ruined melons that looked like red emeralds in the sunlight. But there was another phenomenon at work also, a purple haze in the lee of the mountains, one that smelled of the desert and the end of the season, as though the land wanted to reclaim itself and drive us from its midst.

I FIRED UP THE flatbed and, with Spud in the passenger seat and Cotton behind the cab, headed down the dirt road for the highway, the knob on the floor shift jiggling in my palm.

Spud's face was as coarse as a lampshade and pocked with ringworm scars, his head shaped like an Idaho potato. He always wore a wilted fedora low on his brow, and cut his own hair to save money for brothels. He had been on his own since he was eleven years old. One mile down the road, he unscrewed the cap on a canteen and filled a jelly jar half-full with dago red. "Want a slug?"

I gave him a look.

"Mind if I do?" he said.

"Mr. Lowry entrusted us with his truck."

"A passenger drinking in the truck don't hurt the truck, Aaron."

"Do whatever you want, Spud."

He poured the wine carefully back into the canteen, shaking out the last drop. "Why are you so weird, Aaron? I mean deeply, brain-impaired weird?"

I drove with one hand, the breeze warm on my face, the sky piled with plum-colored clouds above the mountains, backdropped by a molten sun.

"You not gonna say anything?" he asked.

"Nope."

"I know where there's a jenny barn."

"A what?" I said.

"In Kentucky that's what we call a whorehouse. In this particular one, the *señoritas* sing in your ear if you tip them."

I nodded and turned on the radio. Someone had broken off the aerial. I clicked off the radio, my gaze straight ahead. The slopes of the mountains were deep in shadow now, the smell of the sage as dense as perfume.

"Silence is rude, Aaron," Spud said. "Actually, an act of aggression."

"In what way?"

"It's like telling people they've done something wrong. Or they're stupid and not worth talking to."

"You're a good fellow, Spud."

He squeezed his package as though he were in pain. "I guess I'll have to get married again. My last wife hit me upside the head with a skillet and threw me down a fire escape. She was the only one who loved me. My other two were meaner than a bucket of goat piss on a radiator."

Cotton had unrolled his sleeping bag between two stacks of

tomato crates and was reading a Classics Illustrated comic book, his head propped up on a pillow that had no cover on it. His hair was silver and grew to his shoulders, his left eye as white and slick as the skin on a hard-boiled egg. He said during the liberation of Rome, he chased Waffen-SS miles through the catacombs to a chamber under the Vatican Obelisk. There were three levels in the catacombs, and the third level, where the SS had fled, was full of water that had been dripping there for almost two thousand years. He said he had a grease gun and killed every SS in the chamber, the same one where the bones and dust of Saint Paul and Saint Peter lay inside two stone coffins.

Spud saw me looking at Cotton in the rearview mirror. "You believe that war story of his?"

"About the Nazis in the catacombs?"

"Wherever."

"Yeah, I believe him," I said.

"How come you're so certain?"

"Because Cotton doesn't care what people think of him one way or another."

"Did you really study journalism at the University of Missouri?"

"Yep."

"Why are you doing this shit?"

"It's a good life."

He looked at the countryside flying by the window. "I know what you mean. I love slopping pigs and milking cows before breakfast, and chopping cotton from cain't-see to cain't-see. You're a laugh riot, Aaron."

Chapter Two

WE UNLOADED AT a packing house by the tracks outside Trinidad, then blew a tire and decided to stay over, with Mr. Lowry's permission. Not many growers were farming tomatoes anymore, but Mr. Lowry took pride in his produce and yearly rotated his acreage and plowed it with compost and cow manure, and every five years brought in a refrigerated load of waste from a fish cannery on the Texas coast. Afterward, the birds picked his fields like seagulls, and sometimes bears came down from the mountains and tore up the rows, but Mr. Lowry's sliced tomatoes were the fattest in the area and bled like beefsteak.

When we pulled in at the motel, the sun was a spark in the crevice of two mountains, the shadows as long and purple as a bruise. "I'd like to go on a field trip tonight," Spud said.

"This truck is not going to a hot-pillow joint," I said.

"What about you, Cotton?" he said.

"*What* about me?" Cotton said.

"What's your vote?" Spud asked. "You can just sit in the living room if you like. Or—"

"You're always borrowing trouble, Spud," Cotton replied.

The motel we used in Trinidad was clean and cheap and attached to a restaurant with neon cactuses and sombreros and Mexican beer signs scrolled in the windows. The mountains around Trinidad were the deep metallic blue of a razor blade, and seemed to rise straight and flat-sided into the clouds. The wind was balmy from the layer of warm air that lifted at sunset from the plateau at the bottom of Ratón Pass. Trinidad was a magical city in those days, full of brick streets that climbed into the hills and nineteenth-century saloons where Doc Holliday and the Earps probably drank and slept during the 1880s when they were wiping out the remnants of the Clanton gang.

We showered and shaved and put on fresh clothes, then went into the restaurant and ordered plates of tamales and beans and enchiladas and guacamole salad. Four men were standing at the bar, not sitting but standing, the way men do when they have more on their mind than just drinking. I thought maybe they didn't like Cotton's long hair or felt challenged by his jagged profile and one-eyed stare and hunched posture and the slink in his walk and the muscles in his shoulders and upper arms that you associate with a former paratrooper.

Much earlier in my life, I had learned not to make eye contact with the predators who hang in late-night bars, particularly the ones with jailhouse tats who are closet sadists and can't wait to rip a college boy apart. I kept my eyes on my food, then glanced at the bar. The four men were sitting on stools now and watching *Have Gun—Will Travel* on a black-and-white TV.

Spud couldn't keep his eyes off our waitress. Neither could I. Her hair was thick and clean and as bright as a new penny, her skin without a blemish, like the inside of a rose, her legs long and tapered, her pink uniform tight across her rump.

"Y'all want anything else?" she said.

"You from Texas?" I asked.

"I used to be. You gonna have dessert?"

"No, ma'am."

"I will if he won't," Spud said, his eyes lighting. "I'll eat anything that's sweet. With both hands. Any way I can get it. Whatcha got, girl?"

She handed him a menu. "Try reading the list under 'Desserts.'"

She was standing inches from me. Her hip brushed against my shoulder.

"Could I have another Dr Pepper?" I said.

"You bet," she said. "*Ice* cold."

IT WAS DARK when we walked out to the parking lot. Our truck was in the shadows, close by the motel. Spud was picking his teeth. Cotton was licking down the seam on a hand-rolled cigarette. The stars were white and cold and so numerous they looked like refrigerated smoke arching over the mountains and down Ratón Pass into New Mexico. I looked through the front window of the café. Our waitress was writing down the order for a Mexican family in a booth. A little boy was crying in a high chair. She patted his head, then put a coloring book and a crayon in front of him.

"You're not gonna let me borrow the truck?" Spud said.

"Nope," I said.

"Drop me off and I'll find my own ride back."

"Can't do it, partner," I said.

"Like you don't have it on your mind, too?" he said.

"I didn't catch that."

"*Ice* cold," he said. "How old is she? Fifteen?"

She was probably nineteen or twenty, but I didn't want to argue. "I didn't mean to judge you, Spud. I told Mr. Lowry I'd be responsible for his truck, that's all."

"So I'll call a cab."

"Here's a dime," I said.

It was a cheap thing to say. Spud was a good soul, as homely as mud, as socially sophisticated as a dirty sock floating in a punch bowl. But secretly, I knew he was a better man than I. He pulled on his dong. "Well, the heck with it. In the next life, I'm coming back as a dildo."

An eighteen-wheeler went by, the driver shifting down, the air brakes blowing for the long descent down the Pass. The stench from the exhaust stacks seemed to violate the perfection of the ink-black sky and the vaporous coldness of the stars and the symmetry of the lighted houses strung through the hills. Then I knew that something was wrong, and it was not the semi or Spud's lust or my inability to stop thinking about the young waitress.

I saw a sticker on the rear bumper of Mr. Lowry's truck that I hadn't paid attention to before. I saw Cotton's hand move to the side pocket of his jeans, his thumb working at the Buck folding knife he carried. A tall, booted man about my age in a coned-up cowboy straw hat, with girlish hips, was standing five feet from us. Three more men stood behind him, silhouetted against a neon cactus on the café window. They were the same ones we had seen standing at the bar. Each of them held an ax handle. One had a blanket draped over his arm.

"What the hell you guys want?" Spud said.

Then they were on us, our arms hardly in the air before the first blows rained down upon us. I saw Cotton's half-opened knife fall from his hand. I felt a string of saliva and blood whip against the side of my face. I saw Spud's jaw drop and his knees collapse, his arms flop at his sides as if his motors had been cut. I saw a blanket swirl above us, undulating like the wings of a giant stingray. Under the blanket, Cotton's face was pressed against mine, his blind eye luminous, his body trembling with shock, his breath rife with the smell of beer and Mexican food.

When the blows stopped, I heard the four men walking away, one of them talking about Richard Boone, the star of *Have Gun—Will Travel*. I got the blanket off my head and stumbled onto the highway as they drove off. I couldn't make out their license number. A beer can flew from the back window and bounced end over end on the asphalt, all the way down the hill.

Chapter Three

TWO SHERIFF'S DEPUTIES put us in the back of a patrol car, and one gave Spud a towel to cup to his mouth. I thought we were going to a hospital. When I saw the lights of the jail, I rattled the grille. "My friend needs stitches," I said.

"The ER is full-up," the driver said, his eyes in the rearview mirror. He was smiling. "Wreck on the highway."

We were put in different cells in a row separated by bars rather than walls. In the morning we were questioned one by one in a room that had a D ring sunk in the floor, although we were not cuffed to it. The detective who questioned us was tall and impersonal and wore a drooping mustache and cowboy boots and a short-brim Stetson tilted over his eyebrows.

"My name is Wade Benbow," he said to me. "Which one are you?"

"Aaron Holland Broussard."

"You never saw those guys before?" he said.

"No, sir."

"They just came out of the dark and laid into you? No warning?"

"No, sir. No warning."

"No explanation?"

"None."

"You think they mistook you for somebody else?"

This time I didn't reply.

"Hearing problem?" he said.

"I already answered your questions, sir."

The window was open. It was raining, and I could smell the rain and the coldness of the bricks in the street and the water backed up in the storm gutters. The sky was an ink wash. What is the lesson you learn if you've even been in the can? You turn compliance into a religion. I lifted my eyes to the detective. "Sir, I don't know who those fellows were or why they attacked us. That's the truth."

"Fellows?" he said.

"Yes, sir."

"The bumper sticker on your truck probably doesn't endear you to some people here'bouts."

"That's Mr. Lowry's truck. I didn't look at the sticker."

"You work for Jude Lowry?"

"Yes, sir."

"I should have known."

"I don't get your meaning," I said.

"No other grower in Colorado would put a union sticker on his own truck. Does your friend Cotton Williams always carry a knife?"

"Yes, sir. For popping bales and such."

"A couple of customers in the café say he pulled it before the fight got started."

"It wasn't a fight, sir," I said.

"Your friend has a sheet. A homicide in Albuquerque. We don't have all the details yet."

"Cotton?" I said.

The streets were billowing with fog, the stone buildings on the hillsides like ships on the ocean. I couldn't imagine Cotton killing someone other than in a war.

"You've been inside, haven't you?" Benbow said.

I looked at the mist drifting over the windowsill.

"No comment?" he said.

"Jails are like flypaper," I said. "They stay with you wherever you go."

"Got a little bit of temper in you?"

"No, sir."

"Stand up."

"What for?"

"I need to hook you up. You bother me, son. I think you might have a warrant on you."

"I'd appreciate it if you didn't call me 'son.'"

He pulled my left wrist into the small of my back and clapped a cuff around it. The resistance in my arm wasn't intentional, but it was there. "Count your blessings," he said.

AFTER EACH OF us was questioned, we were moved to the last cell on the row. Cotton was sitting on a wood bench, his head on his chest. Spud lay on a steel bunk bolted to the wall, a small battery-powered radio resting on his chest. His bottom lip was cut and puffed out of shape and one cheek swollen the size of a baseball. Carl Belew was singing "Am I That Easy to Forget" on the tiny radio.

"Where'd you get *that*?" I said.

"Gave a guy a dollar for it," Spud said.

"You okay, Cotton?" I said.

"I could use some coffee."

I sat down next to him. "I've got to ask you something."

The rain was blowing hard on a window high above us. The walls of the jail were a pale yellow, and the bare bulbs in the corridor ceiling made shadows like bars on Cotton's face. "So ask me," he said.

"You killed somebody in Albuquerque?" My lips felt weak, as though I couldn't push the words out.

"My son."

"Your—" I said.

"I killed my own boy." He fixed his good eye on me, then dropped his head. "My little boy. That's how I still see him. When he was little and not what he turned into."

Spud sat up on the bunk and clicked off the radio.

"He came home drunk and on drugs and shot me in the lung," Cotton said. "Then he shot at his mother and little sister. He'd been in the state boys' home twice. There wasn't no fixing him."

"I'm sorry, Cotton," I said.

"It ain't your fault. He was never right in the head. It ain't anybody's fault. You get the hand that's dealt to you."

A trusty stopped the food cart by our cell door and slid Styrofoam cups of black coffee and paper plates of hash browns and scrambled eggs through the iron slit in the door. Spud carried them to the bench and put a cup of coffee in Cotton's hand. "The trusty said if we eat up, we can get seconds."

Cotton pressed the back of his wrist in each eye and stared at nothing, a wisp of steam rising from his cup.

That morning mr. Lowry came to the jail and got us released. No effort was made to find out who had attacked us, or at least none that I knew of. Spud had to surrender his battery-operated radio to the deputy from whose desk it had been stolen. Wade Benbow had me brought to his office before I was given back my possessions and allowed to leave the building. He was typing at his desk.

"The waitress at the café left a note for you," he said. He handed me a folded piece of paper.

Another Kind of Eden 19

"What's this about?"

"I wouldn't know. I didn't read it."

The paper had been torn from a spiral notebook. The message was written in pencil: *You don't know what you're dealing with. Call me.* It was signed Jo Anne McDuffy, with a phone number under the name.

"Kid?" Benbow said.

"Sir?"

"Walk away from this. Don't let a bump in the road put you in Cañon City."

Cañon City was the joint. Two busloads of dirty cops in Denver had just been sent there.

He resumed typing as though I were not there.

IT WAS SATURDAY, and the rain was still falling, and clouds of white fog were rising from the downtown storm sewers. Cotton and Spud followed Mr. Lowry back to the farm in the truck, and I stayed in town and called the number Jo Anne McDuffy had given me.

"It's Aaron Broussard," I said inside the phone booth. "Can I see you?"

"See me?" she asked.

"To talk about the fellows who attacked my friends and me. You said to call you."

"I didn't say anything about you seeing me."

"Well, I'd like to, anyway."

"It's not a very convenient time."

"How about tonight?"

"I have to work."

"Miss Jo Anne, I'm no trouble."

"I didn't say you were."

"Who's that?" said a man in the background.

"No one," she answered.

"I can't just walk away from what those fellows did," I said.

"Why do you call them 'fellows'?"

"My father never let me use the word 'guy.'"

She gave me an address. It was several miles outside of town. "When are you coming?" she asked.

"As soon as I can. I don't have a car."

"You say you're no trouble?"

"Not in my opinion," I said.

I hung up and pulled back the folding door on the phone booth. The air was bright with a clean, cold smell like dark water dipped out of a rain barrel in winter, perhaps a harbinger that the gifts of the earth are many, all of them waiting to be discovered.

That probably sounds like a foolish way to think. But youth is its own narcotic, its impermanence our greatest worry and greatest loss. So why put on sackcloth and ashes over the memories we should guard like blue diamonds the rest of our lives?

Chapter Four

SHE LIVED ON a rural road in an adobe-style house with a flagstone porch and a flat roof and cedar logs protruding horizontally from the tops of the walls. There were big shiny-blue ceramic jars on the porch, dripping bugle and clematis vine; an old black Ford pickup was parked in the porte cochere, a fire-engine-red Mustang behind it. I stepped under the porch roof and knocked. The rain-washed paint job on the Mustang seemed the only splash of color in the landscape. She opened the door. "You came here on the deck of a submarine?"

"I thumbed a ride." I saw a man seated behind her at a counter that divided the kitchen and living room. "May I come in?"

"Yeah, sorry," she said. "I'll get you a towel."

Through a side window I could see a picked cornfield, a three-sided shed with pigs in it, a windmill ginning with the pump disconnected, a chain rattling against the stanchions, a gray, tormented sky.

I could feel the man on the counter stool taking my inventory. There is a radar in men that is seldom wrong. I suspect we inherit it from our fellow cave dwellers. You go to shake hands with a man whose benign face and relaxed posture are totally disarming. Then his fingers curl around yours, and a toxin enters your pores and flows up your arm and into your armpit and stays there like a prelude to a heart attack.

"Hi," I said.

"*Ciao,*" he said. His boots were hooked on the stool's rungs. He was tall and lean and wore ironed cargo pants and a leather vest with no shirt, his skin caramel-colored and smooth as clay, his hair long and sun-bleached on the tips, his eyes merry. "That's 'hello' in Italian," he said, and winked.

"No kidding?" I said.

Jo Anne came back with a towel. "This is Henri Devos, my art professor," she said.

"How are you doing?" I said. I took off my raincoat and offered my hand. He did not rise from his stool. He didn't blink, either, the way movie stars don't blink.

"Are you the fellow who had a bad time of it last night?" he said.

"Nothing of historical importance," I said.

"Glad you weren't hurt too seriously. I'd leave the buggers alone."

"I didn't bother the 'buggers.'"

"Bravo! That gives you the moral high ground," he said. "I'd let it go at that."

I nodded, my gaze in neutral space.

"What I mean is they're anachronisms who have no other place to go," he said.

I folded my raincoat and placed it on the floor by the door, my back to him. I was never good at hiding my feelings. "They're victims?"

He grinned, his eyes indulgent, warm, lingering on the edge of kind. He was obviously a pro and not one to take the bait.

"Do I have it right, sir?" I said.

He sniffed and took a breath as though caving in to social necessity. "Their own karma will catch up with them. That's all I was saying. No great message there."

"Like karma caught up with Joseph Stalin?" I said. "Or Hirohito? Boy, those suckers paid the price."

He grinned and looked at Jo Anne. Then I saw it. The flash in the corner of the eye, the deferred longing, the predator that would have to wait for another day. "I have to be going," he said. "But we're on for tomorrow, right?"

"Sure," she said.

"Atta girl," he said. He looked at me. "Can I give you a lift?"

"I can walk," I replied.

"You enjoy sloshing around in stormy weather, splashing through the mud puddles, that sort of thing?"

"Actually, that's why I do farmwork. I don't like to be crowded."

"Sending out warning signals, are we?"

"Does your faculty do student home calls on the weekend?" I said.

"I live not far from here. I dropped by to see how Jo Anne's work is coming along. You don't mind, do you?"

"Stop this," Jo Anne said.

"Let him talk," Devos said. "I have the feeling Aaron is a complex man. Perhaps writing a book on the migrants? Taping folk songs, the John and Alan Lomax routine?"

"Not me," I said. "I have a Gibson guitar and play it badly."

"Oh, humble man."

I could feel a pressure band tightening along the left side of my head. Behind my eyelids, I saw Devos undressing Jo Anne, putting his lips on her breasts, sliding his hand down her stomach. These were the kinds of bizarre images I saw inside my head with regularity; they made me wonder if I was perverse or impaired. The room was swaying. I looked out the window. "Are those the neighbor's pigs?"

"I wouldn't know," Devos said.

"I know everything there is to know about pigs," I said.

"Hamps, Yorks, Hamp-Yorks, York-Hamps, Poland China, Chester Whites, Red Wattles. Let's take a walk out to the pen. You might want to paint them. It's probably cheaper than hiring nude models. Or do you use your students for that?"

"Leave," Jo Anne said to him.

Devos got off the stool and picked up an Australian army campaign hat that rested crown down on the counter. He fitted it on his brow and tightened the chinstrap. "Our friend here is an all-right fellow," he said to her. "He's had a rough go of it, and I can't blame him for his feelings. Give me a ring later, and we'll talk about your new work. It's marvelous."

My stomach was roiling. But the problem wasn't his. I had allowed him to be magnanimous at my expense. He opened the door, then turned and gave her a thumbs-up, the rain blowing a nimbus around his head, wetting his skin, the warmth in his eyes and the sensuousness in his mouth undisguised. I felt like a voyeur.

JO ANNE WATCHED Devos drive away in his Mustang, then slapped a legal pad on the counter and began writing with such intensity and anger that the lead in her pencil broke.

"What are you doing?" I said.

"What does it look like?" She started writing again. "Darrel Vickers led the attack on you. His father's name is Rueben. He's worse than the son. They're both buckets of shit."

"I'm sorry I offended your friend, or whatever he is."

"Don't worry about it."

"Meaning I should toggle along?"

Her face was heated, and she curled her nails into the heels of her hands like someone who wasn't used to getting angry. "Don't go near the Vickers family. You'll lose."

"You're really a painter?"

My words seemed to break on her face. She was wearing tennis shoes without socks and a denim shirt that hung over a frilly white dress printed with wash-faded pink roses. There was a mole by the side of her mouth and freckles on the backs of her hands.

"I lied to your friend about writing a book," I said. "I wrote a novel that has been rejected all over New York."

"Why didn't you tell Henri that?"

"If you have faith in your gift, you don't talk about it with people who've never paid any dues," I said. There was a sun-porch off the living room, an easel by the picture window, a tarnished silver glow in the sky above a mountain that looked made of slag. "Can I see your work?"

"What makes you think Henri has never paid dues?" she said.

"He thinks he's better than other people. Only one kind of person does that: somebody who hasn't gotten his ticket punched."

Her bluish-green eyes were sullen and receded in her face, perhaps because she wanted to show me her art but felt it would be a betrayal of a friend. How do you recognize a real painter or writer? They're monks, no matter what they pretend to be. "I don't like people staring at me," she said.

"I came here because I needed to thank you for coming to the jail," I said. "You're brave, Miss Jo Anne. It's written all over you."

She looked at me uncertainly, her lips parting, her eyes focusing on me as though I were not the same person who had walked in unannounced from a storm and immediately become a harbinger of trouble in her life. She drew in her breath, a flush of color like the petal of a broken red tulip on her throat.

"I've got to make a confession also," I said. "I'm twenty-six and a failed English instructor, and with justification, some people would say I shouldn't be hanging around a girl your age."

"I'll decide who hangs around me and who doesn't."

"Could I look at your paintings?"

"Help yourself."

The light was poor on her sunporch, the barren landscape a playground for dinosaurs, a solitary hill in the distance that resembled a dead volcano, the sun a gaseous imitation.

She walked among her paintings and turned around slowly. The hem of her dress fluttered from the warm air of a floor fan. There was a softness around her mouth that made my heart ache, and I knew I was straying into a situation that was wrongheaded and maybe exploitive.

"I was drying my canvas when Henri came over," she said. "I paint things not many people care about. Maybe they're not that good. Henri is the only one to see them. What do you think?" She picked up a canvas that was propped against the wall and held it up for me to see. "This is one of a dozen on the same subject."

I wasn't ready for it. The intensity and depth of the image made my stomach clench. I wanted to scrub it from my mind so I would not have to view it in my sleep. The canvas had become an entryway into a ragged pit in the earth where eleven children and two women were assembled like a church choir, their heads shaped like darning socks, backdropped by smoke and flames, their mouths black holes, their screams trapped under the paint.

I LOOKED AT EACH of the paintings, all of them an extrapolation from photographs taken after the 1914 Ludlow Massacre just twelve miles up the road: armored cars mounted with machine guns; soldiers in campaign hats armed with Springfield rifles; the body of a dead miner lying by a train track; incinerated shacks, the families bunched in front of them in their best clothes, as though attending a funeral, their meager belongings—a pipe bed frame, a hand-crank laundry tub, a tin bread box, a tricycle, its tires melted—poking out of the ashes.

"Not many people know about the Ludlow Massacre," I said. "At least in Texas, they don't."

"My father talked about it all the time."

"He was a miner?"

"He was a preacher. He was born blind and never saw light except in his sleep. We ran a hotel that was built on the Goodnight-Loving Trail. It looked like a palace." When Jo Anne smiled, I wanted to touch her face.

"Are your folks still living?"

"No, my mother died of cancer, and my father was sucked up from a storm cellar by a tornado. I rode the Greyhound all over the Panhandle looking for him."

"Sorry?"

"I thought maybe the tornado had set him down somewhere and he'd lost his memory, like Moses wandering around in the desert. I spent two years looking for him, then I sold the hotel and came up here and bought this house and enrolled at the junior college." She stopped. "I told you how I feel about people who stare."

"I don't mean to. Can I see you after you get off tonight?"

"No."

"Why not?"

"I'll be tired."

"Can I see you in the morning?"

"Henri is taking me to breakfast."

I felt cold and wet and used up, the moldy stink of the jail still on my skin. I looked at the yellow legal tablet on the counter. "What are the first names of the Vickers family again?"

"Darrel and Rueben."

"They're criminals?"

"Criminals get charged with crimes. The Vickerses don't. Get it?"

I looked again at the first canvas she had shown me. The children's faces seemed to reach across time, begging for help, a kind word, or just an explanation. I could not take my eyes off the painting.

She studied my face. "You all right?"

"Sure," I said.

"No, you're not. You're a strange one."

"I've never had high regard for normalcy."

"Give me a few minutes."

"What for?"

"I'll drive you to wherever you're staying."

Chapter Five

SUNDAY NIGHT I told Spud and Cotton who our attackers were. On Monday morning we had just taken a break from cleaning and harrowing twenty acres, split by a creek lined with cottonwoods, when we saw a dirty yellow race car turn off the two-lane and come hard down the road, troweling a flume of dust so thick it blotted out the sun. The race car was dented and had a big black number 7 painted on the hood and the driver's door.

Mr. Lowry was standing with us under a solitary cotton-wood tree by a creek bed, drinking from a tin cup he'd just filled from our watercooler, one that had a block of ice float-ing under the lid. He was a handsome man with thick white hair and the chiseled features I always associated with the revolutionary soldiers who fought at Breed's Hill. A Rotary Club article in a local newspaper said he had migrated from Massachusetts to Colorado after his return from World War I. The article said he was a recipient of the Medal of Honor. Mr. Lowry never argued or demeaned and reminded me in many ways of my father, who had been at both the Somme and the Marne.

"Who's that?" Cotton said.

"Rueben Vickers and his son," Mr. Lowry said. "We're not going to have trouble with them, are we, Cotton?"

Cotton sipped from his cup, his good eye like a solitary marble on a plate.

"Cotton?" Mr. Lowry said.

"It won't start on my account, Mr. Lowry," Cotton said.

"What about you, Spud?" Mr. Lowry asked.

Spud's eyes were half-lidded. You could never tell what Spud was thinking. Most of the time it was about women. But he came from East Kentucky, and I believed on occasion his thoughts wandered into the dark hollows of his ancestors. "They hurt us pretty bad, Mr. Lowry. It's not fair what they got away with."

"I'm asking if you'll put your trust in me for the next few minutes."

"Yes, sir, if that's what you want," Spud replied.

"What about you, Aaron?" Mr. Lowry said.

The cottonwood leaves were clicking in the sunlight. Mr. Lowry didn't have to wait long for an answer from me. I grew up in Texas and Louisiana and knew better than to mess with rich and powerful people, particularly in the oil business. "You're the skipper, Mr. Lowry," I said.

"Well, good enough, fellows," he said, his gaze lingering on me, perhaps not entirely convinced.

The race car pulled onto the grass and into the shade. Rueben, the father, cut the engine and got out. His son, Darrel, followed, but not until his father had closed the driver's door. Darrel closed his own door quietly, snicking it tight, as though trying not to draw attention. His cheeks and throat were patinaed with soft red stubble, his coppery hair freshly barbered and bright with a light oil. He reached behind the seat and lifted up a coned straw hat and put it on, his face shadowing, as though he had taken on another persona.

"What can I do for you, Rueben?" Mr. Lowry said.

Rueben Vickers was probably no more than five nine and had the wiry muscularity of a man for whom physical work was a religion. He wore sandals and a plain beige short-sleeve shirt and unironed brown slacks that flattened against his body in the wind, the kind of dress a self-made and socially indifferent man would wear every day of the week without remembering he'd put them on. His expression was a different matter. It was a lightning bolt, a permanent emotional disfiguration, the flag of a man who kept the wounds green unto the grave.

"A detective came to our ranch in the middle of dinner," he said. "His name is Wade Benbow. Know him?"

"Seems familiar. What'd he do?" Mr. Lowry said.

"He said somebody here accused my son of attacking your workers," Vickers replied.

I knew then that Jo Anne had given the name of Darrel Vickers to Detective Benbow, because I had not.

"Point out the liar who did that, Jude," Vickers said.

I could hear the tree rustling above us. Cotton was sitting on a stump. He lit a hand-rolled cigarette and blew out the paper match and puffed on the cigarette. The smoke broke apart in the silence. Cotton spat between his legs.

"You have a mark on your face, Darrel," Mr. Lowry said. "Did someone strike you?"

"That man right there, the one with the dead eye," Darrel replied.

Cotton looked asleep, his cigarette hanging between two fingers.

"You, there," Vickers said. "With the Bull Durham."

Cotton cleared his throat and mumbled.

Vickers's face twitched as though a fly had landed on it. "*What* did you say?"

Cotton shook his head as though distancing himself from his own words.

"I asked you a question, boy," Vickers said.

"Go easy there, Rueben," Mr. Lowry said.

Cotton field-stripped his cigarette and let the tobacco and paper blow away, then rose from the stump and looked at Vickers. "That's your son, is he?"

"Who does he look like?" Vickers said. The disjointed glare in his eyes had frozen, as though he knew he had stepped across a line into unknown territory.

"Then you raised a goddamn liar," Cotton said.

Darrel stepped forward. He was taller than his father, his body flaccid, love handles on his hips, his navel showing above his belt buckle. His father took hold of his arm. "Stay put, son. Are the other ones here?"

"This guy just called me a liar, Daddy."

"We'll make sure he regrets it. Do you see the others or not?"

"Those two by the water can," Darrel said.

"I won't allow this, Rueben," Mr. Lowry said.

"My grandparents pioneered the land you're standing on, Jude," Vickers replied. "They were burned to death by the Comanche three miles from here. You will not lecture me, and you will not bring your unions and your politics into the lives of my employees."

"It was the bumper sticker on my truck, wasn't it?" Mr. Lowry said.

"What are you talking about?"

"Your son and his friends punished three innocent men for driving a truck that had a United Farm Workers sticker on it."

"Don't start what you can't finish, Jude," Vickers said.

"Mr. Vickers?" I said.

"*What?*"

"You're wrong," I said.

"Who the hell do you think you are?" he said.

"I think you know the truth," I said. "I also think you hit your son in the face."

"What's your name?" he said.

"Aaron Holland Broussard."

Vickers chewed on the edge of his lip, nodding. "Stay here, Mr. Broussard." He went to his car and dipped his arm between the driver's door and the seat, then marched toward me, a horse quirt in his right hand. Mr. Lowry tried to stand in front of him, but Vickers knocked him aside.

"Don't you hurt that man, Rueben!" Mr. Lowry said at his back, off balance, holding one hand to his chest.

I was standing on a slope. I could hear the other workers stepping away from me. Vickers was coming straight at me, striding out of the sun's brilliance into the spangled shade under the cottonwood, his face a feral knot. I kept my hands at my sides, my eyes on his. I heard Mr. Lowry cry out, but his voice was lost inside a gust of wind that turned the cottonwood tree into a thousand green butterflies.

Vickers slashed the quirt down across my eye and cheek and mouth. Then he hit me again. And again, each blow taking away the pain from the previous blow. I didn't move, not even to raise my arms. I could feel blood sliding out of my hair, and taste salt on my lips, and hear a ringing sound inside my left ear where he had backstroked me.

Mr. Lowry tried to pull the quirt from Vickers's hand, but Vickers shoved him to the ground. "Old man or not, I'll put it to you, Jude," Vickers said.

"Don't touch Mr. Lowry again," I said. "If you do, your life may be forfeit."

Vickers's face was slick with sweat, his breath short, his voice wadded with phlegm. "I can have you in prison for that one remark."

"Cotton is a recipient of the Silver Star, Mr. Vickers," I said. "You owe him an apology."

He backed away from me into full sunlight. His quirt was marbled with my blood. "You won't talk to me like that."

"I think you have a black soul, sir," I said.

He seemed to flinch as if struck by an invisible hand. He turned in a circle, the quirt shaking uncontrollably in his hand. Then he pointed it at me as though he had forgotten where he was. "I can flay you alive."

"You're a bully, Mr. Vickers. I also think you carry an incubus, one that will cost you your soul."

He wasn't ready for it. His face seemed to crumple, like a sheet of paper curling above a flame. His lips were shaking, the top of his exposed chest printed with green veins. He turned to Mr. Lowry. "You'll pay for this, Jude!"

"Get off my land, Rueben," Mr. Lowry said. "Never enter it again."

"This is not over," Vickers said. "No one talks to me like that."

"Aaron is right," Mr. Lowry said. "What you hear is your own evil speaking to you. Be gone with you."

Vickers pushed his son toward the car, then got behind the wheel and started the engine. He ground the gears and backed in a circle and crashed over a rock, his wheels fishtailing and scouring dirt and divots of grass in the air. As the dust thinned and the car spun onto the road, his son's eyes found mine, in the way fellow travelers find each other. I even thought he might show sympathy or offer a kind word. He grinned and mouthed the words "You're fucked."

My face and head felt as though they had been attacked by bumblebees. Mr. Lowry was digging a first-aid kit out of his truck. Spud and a black man eased me down on the tailgate of the truck and put a cup of water in my hand.

"Why'd you let him hit you like that?" Spud said.

"Anybody can fight," I replied.

Spud stared blankly at the blueness of the mountains, the dry creek bed and the white rocks stenciled with dead hellgrammites, the cottonwoods swelling with wind. "What was that stuff about him putting you in prison?" he said.

"Vickers was just making noise."

"You don't think he's coming after us?"

"Not us. We're too obvious."

"What do you mean 'not us'? People like Vickers chew up people like us."

I tried to stand up. Behind my eyelids, I saw Jo Anne on the sunporch of her house, the warm air of the floor fan blowing the hem of her dress. Then I fell sideways as though one of my legs had been chopped off.

Chapter Six

Mr. LOWRY DROVE me to the emergency room at San Rafael Hospital and stayed with me while an intern treated the welts on my face and head and stitched a lesion above my ear.

"Somebody attacked you?" the intern said, dabbing a place above my eye.

"Yes," I said.

"We'll have to report this to the police," he said.

"A man named Rueben Vickers hit me with a quirt."

Showing no reaction, the intern concentrated on the cut, his hand steady. "There," he said. "Come back in five or six days and we'll take your stitches out. It's been nice meeting you." He left the cubicle.

"This grieves me deeply, Aaron," Mr. Lowry said.

"It's not your fault, sir."

"Why didn't you defend yourself?"

"Fear."

"I don't understand."

"I fear what I'm capable of, Mr. Lowry. Sometimes I go to a dark place in my head, and I don't know how to get back."

"How long have you had this condition?"

"Since I was a little boy."

I took off my hospital gown and put on my shirt. Mr. Lowry's eyes were a clear blue, his hair as white as cotton, his skin as soft as a baby's. "You used a term with Rueben that got to him. What do you know about an incubus?"

"It's a form of demon from the Middle Ages."

"I see. You believe in demons?"

"I've seen enough evil in people without looking for the devil."

"After the season, are you going down to the Rio Grande Valley with the other boys?" he asked.

"I'm thinking about it."

"Got a girl on your mind?"

"How'd you know?"

"What young man doesn't?" he said. "Why have you chosen this kind of life for yourself, Aaron?"

"It's the one I do the best," I replied.

The intern pulled back the curtain on the cubicle, the plastic rings rattling. "There's a police detective named Benbow who wants to talk to you," he said.

Detective wade benbow was waiting for us by the emergency entrance. He took off his short-brim Stetson when he saw Mr. Lowry. "How do you do, Mr. Jude? I'd like to talk to Aaron in my vehicle if you don't mind. We won't be long."

"That's fine," Mr. Lowry said.

I sat down in the passenger seat of the unmarked car and left the door partly open. Benbow got behind the wheel. "Close the door," he said.

"Yes, sir."

His eyes roved over my face. "You took quite a licking."

"I've been through worse."

"Where was that?"

"Who cares?" I said.

"Are you pressing charges?"

"No, sir."

He was wearing a gray sport coat and a snap-button purple shirt and a wide leather belt and dark slacks that had flecks of grass on the cuffs. An open package of Lucky Strikes rested on the dashboard. He picked it up and shook a cigarette loose. "Want one?"

"No, thanks."

He tossed the package back on the dash. "Good for you. I'm trying to quit. Want to tell me why you're not pressing charges?"

"I don't trust y'all or anything you do."

"How did you arrive at this great assessment of our system?"

"I was in a lockdown unit fifteen feet from where a man was electrocuted. I could hear him weeping. The electricity made a warm smell, like someone ironing clothes."

Benbow's eyes were empty. My words seemed to have no influence on him. He took a manila folder from the pouch on the door and opened it on the steering wheel. "I have six photographs I want you to see. Give me any thoughts that cross your mind."

The detective's photos were eight-by-ten, black-and-white, the grotesqueness of the images probably accentuated by a Graflex with a flash attachment. But under the best of circumstances, the dead are not cooperative when a camera disrupts their sleep, particularly when their remains have been exhumed in rain-soaked woods or pulled from a drainpipe or a wall or inside a freezer, the light in their eyes sealed with frost.

Detective Wade Benbow's photos were no exception. All of them showed the bodies of women or teenage girls, each with a rictus grin or matted hair or fingernails like knife points, or clothes that would have to be peeled from the skin with tweezers, or eyes that had eight-balled.

"Why are you showing me these photos?" I said.

"I've got a hang-up. I don't like men who kill women and young girls."

"Where'd these murders happen?"

"Within two hundred miles of here, in both Colorado and New Mexico. Over a period of about three years."

"How'd they die?"

"If I tell you, you'll wish I hadn't."

"I don't understand why you're singling me out."

He leaned across the seat and removed an envelope from the glove box and took a color photo of a little girl from the envelope. She was smiling and had braces and bright yellow hair. A grape sno-cone was clutched in her hand; her cheeks were red and looked heated, as though she had just come from play.

"Who is she?" I said.

"My granddaughter. She was twelve years old. Her body was found south of Pueblo."

"I'm sorry."

"Before the run-in at the café, you never had any contact with Darrel Vickers?"

"Not that I remember."

"Say again?"

"I have blackouts."

"That's a little different from what you told me before."

"Sir, I'm done with this."

"Would you like to see the picture of my granddaughter when she was lifted out of an oil tank?"

"I'm not the cause of your problem."

"I'm glad you cleared that up for me." He slipped the photo back in the envelope, his fingers shaking. "Darrel Vickers lived with his mother in Denver when he was a child. A girl on the next street was asphyxiated in an abandoned refrigerator. Darrel was seen with her a few hours earlier."

"Why do you keep telling me about Darrel Vickers?"

"Because I think Darrel killed the little girl. Because I know he and his friends are muling dope from the border. Because I want you to wear a wire."

"I won't do it."

"That's your final word?"

"Want me to write it in the dust on your dashboard?"

"Get out of my car."

MR. LOWRY TOLD me to take three days off with full pay and dropped me off in his big Buick at Jo Anne's house. He stuck a twenty-dollar bill in my shirt pocket.

"What's that for?" I asked.

"Get yourself some fresh clothes and take your girlfriend to dinner and a movie."

"You don't have to do that, Mr. Lowry."

"You're a good boy, Aaron. So is Spud and so is Cotton. Fellows like you are the salt of the earth. Don't let anybody tell you different."

Then he drove away. I walked up into the shade of Jo Anne's porch. I had called earlier but had mentioned nothing about my encounter with Rueben Vickers. Yesterday I had taken Jo Anne to breakfast, then had returned to the Lowry farm. I probably hadn't spent more than an aggregate of three hours with her. I had not even held her hand. Yet I felt I had known her for years. Know the song "Born to Be with You" by the Chordettes? I couldn't get it out of my head. I wanted to hold her against me. I wanted to smell her hair and kiss her neck. I wondered if I was going crazy.

She must have seen me out the window. She jerked open the door. "What happened to you?"

"I straightened out Rueben Vickers and his son. Mr. Lowry said I should take you to dinner and a movie."

"You look like you climbed out of a concrete mixer."

Before I could answer, she pulled me inside, glancing back at the two-lane state road as she shut the door.

"What's going on?" I asked.

"My boss called this morning and said he had to let me go."

"Why?"

"My art classes cause too much conflict with my schedule. It's a lie."

"Did you tell him that?"

"What do you think? He said I was a 'good girl' and he didn't want to hurt my feelings."

I sat down at the counter. The furniture in her living room was made of leather and sanded driftwood, the rug woven with a black-and-red-and-blue Indian design. Everything about her house was immaculate. I wondered how any grown man with a teaspoon of charity or self-respect could do such harm to such a good young woman.

"Does your boss know Rueben Vickers?" I asked.

"I don't know."

"I'd like to talk with him."

"My boss? Stay away from him."

"You lost your job because of me. What's his telephone number?"

"Right now I'm eligible for unemployment. Don't piss him off. He'll challenge my application. You want a beer or a soda?" She opened the icebox door and bent over and began rattling bottles and cans around. She was wearing a long-sleeve black western shirt with roses on it and a braided cloth belt and baggy blue jeans that exposed her baby fat. "Did you hear me? What do you want to drink?"

"A soda," I said, the words tight in my throat.

She uncapped a Coca-Cola for me and a Tuborg for herself. She tilted the bottle to her mouth, the sunlight through the window sparkling inside the amber glass, the foam sliding down her throat. There was something wrong in the image, though, like a painting that contains one incongruous detail. She blew out her breath. "Shit," she said.

"Shit, what?"

"Everything. It's harder looking for a job than working. How's your face feel?"

"Fine."

"You don't drink?"

"I used to."

"But you don't now?"

"Alcoholism runs in my family."

She came around the counter and sat down next to me. "You need to get honest with me, Aaron."

"How's that?"

"You're not a picker or a ranch hand. You're on the run from the law or maybe a wife and baby or something that's a whole lot bigger than you. That's what I think."

"I'm not on the run from anybody," I said.

She drank from the bottle again. I could smell the beer on her breath. I wanted to put my mouth on hers.

"Are you married?" she said.

"No."

"Guys with master's degrees get it on with waitresses. They don't marry them."

I looked at her fingers curved around the beaded moisture on the Tuborg label. "You didn't buy that."

"What are you talking about?"

"Young women just getting by don't keep imported beer at home unless a man buys it for them. That's the professor's Tuborg, isn't it?"

"What if it is?"

"I think he's a predator."

She took another sip from the bottle. "Here we go again."

"You told him you were fired?"

"Yes," she said, her eyes going away from mine.

"Did he want to talk to your employer?"

"Like I said, it wouldn't do any good. It would just cause harm."

"Did he ask if he could?"

"No."

She went to the sink and poured the beer down the drain, then dropped the bottle in a trash bag under the sink. "You sure know how to rain on the parade. Even when there's no parade to rain on."

"When you let me in, you looked out at the road like you were worried."

"I don't remember."

"You think Rueben Vickers might be sending someone out here?"

"It's a very good possibility."

"I feel bad about what's happened to you, Jo Anne."

"Come here."

"What for?"

She ripped an ice tray from the freezer compartment and dropped it into the sink. "Get the ice cubes out. I'll get a towel and a rolling pin from the pantry. Give me any more trouble and I'll use the rolling pin on your head."

SHE CRUSHED THE ice cubes inside the towel, then tightened and retied the corners of the towel and walked me into her bedroom and pushed me down on the pillow and sat beside me and touched her improvised ice bag to the welts on my face and head. Then she stroked my forehead and cheek and eyebrows. Her fingers were as light and cool as refrigerated air, and she did something no girl or woman had ever done to me before. She leaned over and kissed each of my eyelids and my mouth, then continued to stroke my hair with her nails until I felt myself drifting away, free of all pain and age, free of the evil that undid Eden and set brother against brother and left us forever wounded and benighted and at war with ourselves and the earth.

I wanted to reach up and hold her, but she didn't allow me to. She got beside me and held my head against her breast and hummed a song as though comforting a child. I saw myself descending into a garden filled with palm and orchid and fruit trees and animals and flamingos and swans and herons and parrots and peacocks whose fanned tails were embroidered with purple and green eyes that seemed as numerous as the stars but made no judgment of us.

I could feel her thighs spread on either side of mine, feel her hand place me inside her, and feel her breath against my ear, her tongue in my mouth, her hands trembling on my face when we both came.

I dropped away into a place I never wanted to leave, and did not wake until the sun faded and died like thunder in the hills and hailstones clattered on the hardpan as far as the eye could see.

Chapter Seven

I WROTE JO ANNE a note and left early in the morning, ashamed that I had caused her to lose her job and dragged her into a dangerous world occupied by men like Rueben Vickers. And rather than arrive at her house as benefactor and friend, I had become the pitiful victim upon whom she had to take mercy when she owed me nothing and I had nothing to give her in turn.

I walked and hitched a ride to the bank in Trinidad where I had saved up almost six hundred dollars. I withdrew it all and closed the account, then took a city bus to a used-car lot and paid two hundred dollars for a salt-eaten 1952 Chevrolet. It had no radio or heater; the paneling inside the doors was cardboard. The owner of the car lot, Put-Some-South-in-Yo'-Mouth Fat Johnny Dean, also owned the diner and the pawnshop across the street. After the paperwork, he walked me to the car and opened the driver's door. "We have a scavenger special every day," he said. "Tell your friends."

I rubbed the spray of rust on the hood. "I think I saw this car in Galveston. After the last hurricane."

He crimped his mouth, his face reddening, like he had stopped breathing. Then his mouth burst open, his eyes watering while he slapped his thighs. "You don't like the way it drives, come back and I'll give you a shovel to bury it."

I looked across the street at the pawn store. "What have you got in the way of sidearms?"

He wiped at his eyes. "You're serious?"

"I can go thirty-five dollars for a quality piece."

His eyes held mine. The humor had gone out of his face. "You want a gun for personal protection?"

"Maybe."

"Follow me. Watch the traffic. People tend to run the light."

Five minutes later, he placed four pistols on the glass top of his display counter. I picked up a .38 snub-nose Police Special and released the cylinder and rotated it and looked through the barrel, then snipped the cylinder back into the frame. The bluing was worn, the wood grips grainy and dark with oil, but there was no pitting inside the barrel, and the cylinder locked solidly in place when I cocked the hammer.

"How much?" I said.

"I need to get fifty on it."

"Thirty-five is all I can afford."

He fed a stick of gum into his mouth and shook his head. "Cain't do it."

"Forty for the gun and a box of shells."

He smacked his gum, his eyes on mine. "You look like you walked into a window fan."

"So?"

"You scare me. You fixing to do some payback?"

"I got a rodent problem."

He started to drag the revolver off the counter.

"There are people out there who'd like to put me in a box," I said.

"Son, I don't know who you are, but you sure know how to put a blister on a man's conscience."

I DROVE TO JO Anne's house, but she wasn't home. I put one hundred dollars and a note in an envelope and slid it under the door. The note read: *I hope this will tide you over.* I bought clothes and a toothbrush and toothpaste and a razor and checked in to a motel at the top of Ratón Pass. I peeled back the covers on the bed and lay facedown without undressing and fell instantly asleep, one arm touching the floor, one hand clutching the .38 Special under a pillow, each chamber loaded with a hollow-point.

I never liked sleep. It took me to too many bad places. Late at night, my parents fought when my father came home from the icehouse, feeling his way along the wall to their bedroom door, which my mother kept closed when he was drinking. Their words were muffled, like shards of anger rising and falling inside a pool of dark water. After I grew older and lost my best friend, Saber Bledsoe, at Pork Chop Hill and my father in a car accident, I knew that sleep would always be my enemy, forcing me to look at images that may have been dreams or, chillingly, replications of real events that took place during one of my blackouts.

I mentioned earlier that they were not chemically induced. Sometimes during a blackout, I got my hands on alcohol and went genuinely insane, shouting at people in the street, once getting into it with Green Berets in a Lake Charles roadhouse, once fighting with cops. In the aftermath, I would be terrified at the fate I could have suffered. My darkest hours came when I was in a deep sleep and a motion picture projector clicked on and lit up a screen inside my head I couldn't flee.

The worst images on that screen showed Saber on a godforsaken hillside in July '53 writhing inside a burst from a Chinese flamethrower, his mouth wide, as though he were calling out to me, his arms extended, begging me to take him home.

I SHOWERED AND SHAVED and called Jo Anne in the morning. "Hey," I said.

"Hey," she replied.

"Can you have breakfast with me?"

"I have to look for a job. I won't be able to get compo."

"Compo?" I repeated.

"Unemployment compensation. My boss says I quit. It'll take two months for me to get a hearing."

"Did you get the envelope I put under the door?"

"Yes, that's nice, Aaron. But I can't take it."

"You have to."

"No, I do not."

When I entered puberty and the problems that go with it, my father gave me a brief admonition on the subject and never spoke about it again: "Women are God's greatest creation. So are young girls. No matter what they do, never show them disrespect. When you find one who won't give up her principles at gunpoint, never let go of her."

"When can I see you?" I said. "I have to be back at the farm by tomorrow evening."

"Aaron, I hope I haven't misled you."

"I don't understand," I said, my heart sinking.

"I have ties to Henri."

"What if I drop by his office and tell him he's untied?"

"That's not your choice to make."

"I think he's a bum. Not like the bums I've met on freight cars, just a bum."

"I can't believe the way you talk about people."

But I could tell she was on the edge of laughing, and I felt like flowers had just bloomed all over my motel room. "Hey," I said.

"Hey, what?"

"You've got to have dinner with me tonight. I bought a car. A scavenger special."

"A what?"

"I'll cruise by at six."

I CHANGED THE OIL in the Chevrolet and filled the tank and wiped the inside clean and drove to the Mexican restaurant from which Jo Anne had been fired. The lunch crowd was just drifting in, the owner guiding them to tables and handing out menus. He wore a dark blue suit with stripes in it and a soft lavender dress shirt and a plum-colored tie and a red carnation in his lapel. His teeth were small, like kernels of white corn, his black hair shiny and swept up in a pile, his eyes feverishly attentive to his waitresses, his fingers snapping when need be. I walked up behind him. "Could I speak with you, sir?"

His eyes locked on mine. "What do you want?"

"Jo Anne McDuffy didn't quit her job. Why do you want to mess her up with the state employment system?"

"I'll call the police," he said.

Over his shoulder, I recognized a familiar face. Darrel Vickers was eating at the bar, one cheek puffed with food, chasing it with a Lone Star, a big bubble of foam swelling against the inside of the bottle. He was wearing striped pants tucked inside hand-tooled multicolored Mexican stovepipe boots. He shot me the bone.

I looked back at the owner. "Why didn't you call the cops when Darrel Vickers and his friends attacked us?" I said.

He went to the counter and picked up the phone and dialed zero, his eyes never leaving me. Then he turned his back and began talking into the receiver.

I went out the door. The day was cool and bright, the wind

blowing the way it does on the Southern Colorado Plateau at the end of summer, a passenger train dipping into Ratón Pass, its wheels locked for the long, screeching ride down the tracks into New Mexico. Behind me I heard someone coming across the gravel, but I didn't turn around. "Wait up, asshole," a voice said.

I kept walking.

"Hey, dipshit, want to save yourself some trouble?" the same voice said.

I opened my car door and started to get in.

Darrel Vickers kicked the door shut. "I'm doing you a favor, queer-bait."

I brushed the paint where his boot had scratched it. "I thought we were friends."

"You went someplace inside my father that can cost you pain you can't imagine."

I dusted off my fingers. "My remark about an incubus? Yeah, I've given that some thought. I was mistaken. See, an incubus is a male demon that gets inside a woman. A succubus is a female demon that gets inside a man. Your father has a succubus. Tell him I'm sorry for the mix-up."

"Listen, shit-for-brains, my father boxed Golden Gloves and turned a kid into a vegetable. He killed a guy on the racetrack doing a hundred and ten miles an hour. He finished the last lap without slowing down. What's that tell you?"

"You attacked us because we had a union sticker on our bumper?"

"Because I fucking felt like it, toe jam."

"Does your father knock you around?"

He pointed his finger in my face. "I can hurt you, man. Not *me,* but people I know, people who do it with pliers."

"I believe you."

"You got something going with Jo Anne McDuffy?" He had

shaved since I'd seen him at Mr. Lowry's farm, and had clipped his sideburns. "I asked you a question. You think you can come to town and take any girl you want?"

"Your old man get her fired or did you?"

"I wouldn't do that."

"Somebody did."

He removed his hat and gazed down the Pass, then replaced it. "Maybe I could get her a job."

"She might appreciate that."

"Yeah?"

I shrugged.

"What's with you, man?" he said.

"Nothing."

"I don't get it. The way you stood there while my father cut you up with the quirt. What the fuck is with that?"

"I have to go, Darrel. Regarding that business about the succubus?"

"I don't like to talk about that kind of stuff." He shifted his weight, the gravel compressing under his feet.

"Your father and the owner of this restaurant don't need a succubus," I said. "They work for the Prince of Darkness. That's not a shuck, Ace. For real."

His lips parted. He was still standing there when I drove away.

Chapter Eight

I FELT BAD ABOUT it. That night I took Jo Anne to dinner down the Pass in Ratón. Afterward, we drove out on the hardpan and looked at the sweep of the stars arching over the Great American Desert, disappearing beyond the blackness of the mountains in the north. I told her I had talked to her employer about his dishonesty, and I also told her I had dumped a cup of fishhooks inside Darrel Vickers's head.

"My boss can't act any worse than he has," she said. "That business with Darrel is different. He used to come around."

We were sitting in the Chevrolet, in a roadside park not far from the entrance to a horse ranch that had no buildings on it, only windmills and stock tanks and horses nickering in the sun's afterglow. " 'Come around' how?" I asked.

"Calling me up, hanging around the restaurant, following me home. He had it in for Henri, too. He called him a cradle robber in front of people at the college."

I moved closer to her and put my hand on the back of her neck. She closed her eyes and leaned her head back and moved her neck back and forth against my hand. Her skin was warm, her hair soft on the backs of my fingers. I wanted to kiss her, but I was feeling guiltier and guiltier about my behavior. I was a hypocrite. I had taken her employer to task for wronging a fine girl, forgetting that our differences in age and education had not deterred me from accepting the gift of Jo Anne's body. As I had these thoughts, I longed for her again.

"Jo Anne?"

She opened her eyes. A gate on a cattle guard was tinkling in the wind, the horses blowing in the grass. "What?"

"Think I'm taking advantage of you?"

"You're about to get a slap."

"Oh?"

"*Oh,* my foot. Talk down to me like that again and see what happens."

"Yes, ma'am," I said.

She picked up my hand and folded her fingers inside mine. "You don't have to worry about me, Aaron. You're a good soul. It's in your eyes. But you don't know your own mind. I think that's going to bring you a lot of grief."

"It'll be my grief, then."

"You've stirred up Rueben Vickers," she said. "He tried to take me home once."

"Rueben Vickers? Not the son?"

"He was waiting outside the restaurant at two in the morning. He said he wanted to give me a ride. That a storm was coming."

"What happened?"

"I told him no thanks, I had my own car."

"That was it?"

"The next day the state police found a barmaid's body outside Clayton. Her neck had been broken. She'd also been raped."

"Clayton is more than a hundred miles from Trinidad."

"I need to go home, Aaron. I don't feel well."

BUT OUR EVENING wasn't over. Up the Pass, between two craggy, steep-sided mountains, were the ruins of a Spanish-style church with a small bell tower. The stucco walls were yellow in the moonlight, and the ceiling had caved in, and tall deep-green pine trees had grown out of the rubble inside. "You know what that is?" Jo Anne said.

"A Jesuit mission?"

"It was paid for by John D. Rockefeller in 1917, three years after his goons killed the miners at Ludlow. My father would never let us buy gasoline from a Standard Oil filling station."

"Your dad must have been quite a fellow," I said.

"I think one day he's coming back. I still can't believe he's gone."

I looked at her, even though I shouldn't have taken my eyes off the road. She was staring at my headlights tunneling up the canyon, her face transfixed. "Jo Anne?"

"What?"

"Are you okay?"

"I'm tired."

"I have to be back at Mr. Lowry's tonight. Would you mind if I hang around a little while before I head up the road?"

"I've got to clear my head, Aaron."

"Sure," I said.

"I'm sorry."

Not as much as I, I thought.

We didn't speak the rest of the way to her house.

I WOKE EARLY THE next morning and went into the dining hall with Cotton and Spud and sat down for a big breakfast of eggs and biscuits and bacon and any kind of juice and cereal we wanted. Mr. Lowry and his red-haired, jolly Irish wife fed their employees right. Plus, Mrs. Lowry, with her South Boston accent, always had a good word for everyone in the serving line.

She also had the fresh, clean smell of a strawberry cake. No one used profanity in her dining hall. Some of the Mexican families leaned toward one another and said grace. In the coolness of the morning and the softness of the light and the white clouds bunched on the royal-blue magnificence of the mountains, I wondered if the earth could be any better.

I also wondered if this plateau high above the Great American Desert wasn't more than just the earth, in the same way you wonder sometimes if we are not already inside eternity. I wondered if the columns of sunlight spearing through the clouds on the hillsides and the meadows and the dairy barns and the freshly plowed acreage and the cottonwood trees along the stream were not indeed the pillars of heaven, rising into a kingdom where our predecessors were at work and play in the fields of the Lord.

"What are you thinking about?" Cotton asked. He was sitting across from me, eating scrambled eggs with a spoon, his palm wrapped around the handle.

"I guess we're bucking bales today," I said.

"You're not thinking about that waitress, are you?" Spud asked. Both of them were grinning now.

"I can't remember *what* I was thinking about," I said.

"Right," Spud said. "The preacher at our church used to call that impure thoughts. He was the same preacher who baptized me by immersion in the Cumberland River and was so drunk he dropped me in the current. A colored woman in the bulrushes pulled me out with a fishnet. That's a true story."

"You and Moses?" I asked.

"I'm glad you caught that," he said. "Us Caudills have friends in high places."

Cotton took out his cigarette papers and a bag of Bull Durham and cupped a single paper with his index finger and poured tobacco into it. He wet the glue along the rim and rolled the trough into a tight tube and put it in his mouth. "When do you get your stitches out?"

"Three or four more days."

"Word of caution?" he asked.

"Go ahead."

"The Vickerses will get theirs down the line," he said. He struck a paper match and lit his cigarette, his eyes on mine.

"You mean I shouldn't go after them?" I asked.

He blew out the match. "I didn't say nothing one way or the other."

"Then what did you mean, Cotton?"

"Everybody gets the same six feet of dirt in the face. There's some need it earlier than others." He opened a Classics Illustrated comic book he had just bought and began reading. Spud's eyes were as big as quarters.

Chapter Nine

Pᴇᴏᴘʟᴇ ᴡʜᴏ ᴀʀᴇ unknowledgeable about agriculture often refer to farm labor as unskilled. Take bucking bales. Try inserting your fingers inside the twine on ninety pounds of compacted grass after it has been rained on, then flinging it up on the flatbed of a truck and repeating the process every four minutes for eight hours. If you want to up the ante, do it in an electric storm.

That's not all that's involved. Second-cut hay is usually high-octane and can cause pasture bloat in your cows. Bad grass can also sour their milk. Red clover can give Angus the scours or what is called the bloody shits, whichever term you prefer. That said, and all science aside, if you want sciatica or a slipped disk or a double hernia, there is no better way than bucking bales to fix yourself up proper.

Cotton and Spud and I were stacking them four layers high on a flatbed truck driven by a tiny Japanese woman who, regardless of the weather, always wore baggy blue jeans and a denim coat with a scarf tied under her chin and, for extra protection, sunglasses and a straw hat. She wore so many clothes and hats and scarves, I wasn't actually sure what she looked like.

The breeze was cool and warm at the same time, the leaves on the cottonwoods turning gold and flickering in the sunlight, the shadows of sparrow hawks gliding across the pasture. I wondered if Eden had been like this. I also wondered if the founders of our country had this very scene in mind when they envisioned the agrarian republic. And I wondered if they regretted staining it, just as Eden had been stained, when they placed a portion of the human family in shackles and chains and murdered unknown numbers of indigenous people.

I guess these are strange thoughts to dwell upon, but they were the thoughts I was having when I saw Detective Benbow in his unmarked car with two cruisers coming up the dirt road, thumping across the wood bridge over the stream that rippled as clear as green Jell-O through the entirety of Mr. Lowry's property.

Spud took off his hat and wiped his face with an oversize bandana, one of several he'd bought down on the border. He was shirtless, his fat shiny with sweat and flecks of hay. "It's that same cocksucker, isn't it?"

"Lay off the language, Spud," I said. "This isn't the time for it."

"I know what's going on," he replied. "They get you once, they get you for all time. They keep their foot on the neck of the little people."

He took his shirt off the taillight of the truck and popped it on his chest and back, drying and cleaning his skin, then put it on and buttoned it. The unmarked car and two cruisers turned off the dirt road and came toward us, the grass whipping under their bumpers.

Detective Benbow got out of his car and crooked a finger at Spud. "Over here," he said.

"What for?" Spud said.

"Because I said so."

"I didn't do anything," Spud said. One of the deputies started toward him. "Okay, you win," Spud said. "I'm coming."

Benbow was wearing his Stetson hat and a white dress shirt

with puffed sleeves and a dark vest and black trousers; his lean face was unshaved, his eyes tired. In the patches of sunlight and shadow, he looked like a frontier marshal. He yawned and gazed at the hills on the far side of the Lowry house. "Want to tell me about your legal troubles in Kentucky?"

"I didn't have any legal troubles in Kentucky," Spud replied. "Least not more than kid stuff."

"You were in the reformatory?"

"Ninety days in the county jail." He twisted his bandana on the corners, blinking, looking at nothing.

"Why were you in the county jail?"

"A misunderstanding."

"When did child molestation become a misunderstanding?" Benbow said.

"It wasn't any such thing."

"What would you call it?"

"This girl and me were in the motion picture. She was fifteen and I was sixteen. I put my hand in the wrong place and she made a big deal out of it."

"Where were you two nights ago?"

Spud squinted. "I get my days mixed up. Ciphering was never my strong suit."

"You don't remember what you did night before last?"

"I went into Trinidad for a little R and R."

"Getting your ashes hauled? I'd believe that."

"Having a few beers," Spud said, his chin in the air.

Benbow stared at the ground thoughtfully, his thumbs in his belt. "Where in Trinidad?"

Spud gave the name of a pool hall. The woman driving the flatbed cut the engine and got out of the cab. Her nickname was Maisie. She was Nisei Japanese and had been in an internment camp during the war. "What wrong?" she said.

Benbow ignored her. "Were you looking to get even with somebody?" he said to Spud.

"Not me," Spud said, jerking on the ends of his bandana.

"You nervous about something?"

"I don't like people calling me a child molester."

"I had a talk with the sheriff's office in Hazard, Kentucky," Benbow said. "The sheriff told me you got it on the brain."

"What on the brain?"

"*It.*"

Spud looked away as though he wanted to will himself across the fields and into the mountains. He tied the bandana around his neck.

"He good man," the Japanese woman said. "He don't hurt nobody."

Benbow smiled at her, then turned back to Spud. "Know a fellow named Rizzo Marx?"

"No."

"He's the inmate who stole a transistor radio off a deputy's desk and sold it to you for one dollar. Two nights ago somebody flattened all four of his tires behind that same pool hall in Trinidad. Most likely with an ice pick."

"There's a lot of bad people here'bouts, all right," Spud said, looking into the distance.

"The same night a wino saw a man walking on the next block with his arm in a sling. He had a big cardboard box under his other arm. A woman stopped to help him, and the two of them walked off. You weren't in Trinidad then?"

The wind gusted, causing the brim of Spud's hat to tremble like a tobacco leaf.

"The same woman was found in an alley about four the next morning," Benbow said. "Her panties were around her ankles. Her blouse and one shoe were pulled off. She was obviously raped.

I won't tell you what was done to her face. We can't tell the cause of death yet, because too many things could have done it."

Spud looked seasick.

"You don't know anything about it?" Benbow said.

"No, sir."

"But you were in the poolroom?"

"Early. For just a few games of pool."

"Did you vandalize the man's tires?"

"I got nothing to say on that."

"Will your arm fit in that bandana?"

"This ain't right," Spud said, shaking his head. "Nosirree, it ain't right."

"Did you vandalize the vehicle behind the poolroom?" Benbow said. "Establish your credibility. Get in front of this."

"If I say I did, you'll try to hang a murder rap on me."

"Maybe I'm on your side," Benbow said. "You think of that?"

Before Spud could reply, Maisie charged into the circle. "He here every night!" She pointed to her eye. "I see him here! You stop making up stories about good man!"

The second deputy took her by the arm and pushed and pulled her to the truck cab while she hit at him with her free hand. He stuffed her in the driver's seat. But the opportunity had been lost for Detective Benbow. Spud had gotten control of his fear and shame and obviously was not going to be tricked into making an admission that could keep him in jail for months because he couldn't make bail. Benbow opened and closed his right hand, his cheek ridging.

"Detective?" I said.

"Whatever it is, I'm not interested," he said.

"You've got Spud wrong," I said. "Why are you doing this, sir?"

"Some crazy-ass guy known as Bible-thumping Bob called

me up and said you told Darrel Vickers his father worked for the Prince of Darkness. Darrel told his father, and his father beat the shit out of him for not beating the shit out of *you*. Does that make you happy?"

"Why is the preacher reporting to you about the Vickers family?"

"I'm a half inch from hooking you up, son."

"Try it. I've given up on my pacifist beliefs."

"Are you after Jude Lowry's money? Is that why you're here?"

I stepped back from him. I felt a surge of bile in my stomach and saw a flash of light behind my left eye and heard a whirring sound in my ears, an old prelude to a state of mind whose aftermath could steal my sleep for years.

"You got nothing to say?" he asked.

"I'm going to walk away," I said.

"You're going to do what?"

"I think you're a man who can't deal with mirrors, Detective Benbow, and a son of a bitch on top of it."

I walked toward the bunkhouse. He caught up with me and grabbed me by the shirt. A warm breeze was blowing out of the south, yet the sunlight felt cold on my skin and the sun's glare like a laser in my eyes. "Be advised," he said. "You get a free pass this time. Sass me again and I'll fix it so you're a long-term visitor at our gray-bar hotel chain."

Chapter Ten

THAT EVENING MR. Lowry sent word that he wanted to see me. As I walked up the slope to the Victorian home where he and Mrs. Lowry lived, there was a chill in the air, a dimming of light in the hills, as though the season were unfairly shutting itself down. The house was two and a half stories high, painted battleship gray, with verandas and small balconies and lightning rods and weather vanes and dormer windows, the glass coppery with the sun's last rays, and, most oddly, towers with round peaked roofs you would expect to see only on a medieval castle.

Just above the front steps, an American flag hung from a staff that protruded in an upward angle from an eagle-shaped brass socket screwed into a wood pillar on the gallery. I twisted the bell on the door. Mr. Lowry opened it in under five seconds, as though he had been looking through the window. Past the hallway, I could see firelight flickering on the deep leather couches and stuffed chairs and wood furniture in the living room. I had never been inside his home. The floor creaked like a mausoleum's.

"Thank you for coming up, Aaron," he said. "I thought you might be visiting a certain young lady in Trinidad."

"I was fixing to, unless you need me for something."

"I'd just like you to have some cake and coffee with me."

"That's good of you, sir," I said.

I followed him into the living room. A glass table was set with a coffee service and a chocolate cake that had already been cut, the white icing cracked by the knife blade, the slices bleeding with torn cherries. Through a side door, I could see a big desk and a heavy wood chair, a lamp with a green-tinted glass shade on the ink blotter, the shelves on the walls lined with books.

"How is Spud doing?" he asked.

"A little in the dumps."

"I don't blame him," Mr. Lowry said. He pointed for me to sit down, in a kind rather than authoritarian way. "Wade Benbow has been unfairly hard on you boys. There's a reason for it, but not a good one." He watched my expression to see if I understood. His wife looked at me from the kitchen door, then stepped out of the light before I could lift my hand to say hello.

"You know about the death of Wade's granddaughter?" Mr. Lowry said.

"Yes, sir, he told me."

"Did he tell you it was a homicide?"

"Yes, sir, up by Pueblo."

"They were at a picnic. The little girl wandered off when Wade was supposed to be watching her. Someone found her in an oil storage tank after sunset. The cap was probably left open by the maintenance man."

"It wasn't the work of a serial killer?"

"People believe what they need to," he said. "Wade isn't the exception."

I tried not to look at my watch. But he read my mind. "Have one cup of coffee and I'll let you go."

He poured some into a cup before I could respond, his face tight, a nervous twitch in his hand.

"Mr. Lowry, can I help you with something?"

"Yes, you can. I need a new foreman. The pay is a hundred eighty-five dollars a week, plus your board."

"I don't know as I'd qualify," I said.

"Well, I asked you here this evening for another reason, too. I think you carry a burden of some kind. My boy did the same thing. He brooded and brooded, and rather than share his secret, he lied about his age and joined the army. He died at Guadalcanal when he was seventeen."

I didn't know what to say. I didn't want to talk about myself, and an apology for the death of his son twenty years ago seemed an insult to his ability to accept loss. I apologized anyway.

But he wouldn't let go. "What bothers you, Aaron?"

"A psychiatrist said I have a personality disorder," I said, and tried to smile. "In my case that means multiple personalities."

"I know what it means."

"It's just the way I am, sir."

He got up from the couch and went to the mantel. He returned with a framed photo. In it a soldier was wearing a field jacket and a steel pot with a camouflage cover on it; he carried a puppy on his shoulder. "That's our son," Mr. Lowry said.

"He's a fine-looking fellow," I said.

"He bears a strong resemblance to you."

I didn't see it, but I didn't want to contradict him.

"He caused a girl to have an abortion. Do you know what bothers me most? Somehow he thought he had to be perfect in my eyes. I laid that cross on the shoulder of my own son."

He put the picture back on the mantel. "Think it over about the job. The life of a rambling man is fun when you're young. Down the track, it can get mighty tiresome. Ask Cotton Williams."

"I have holes in my memory, Mr. Lowry. I dream about

things that maybe I did but can't remember. I don't trust myself or know who I am. I think maybe I've done really bad things."

"Know what faith is?" he said.

"I can't really say."

"It amounts to believing others when they tell you you're a good fellow. Give that some thought."

I FINISHED MY COFFEE and shook hands with Mr. Lowry and went outside. I didn't get far. Mrs. Lowry was waiting for me in the shadows. She was wearing a white dress with big pink roses printed on it, her dull-red hair piled in swirls on her head. "I heard everything in the kitchen," she said.

"I hope I didn't say anything wrong."

"Can I put in my two cents?"

"Yes, ma'am," I said.

"You have such good manners. You had a good upbringing."

"That's very nice of you, Mrs. Lowry."

"That's not the two cents I had to put in."

"Oh."

"He thinks the world of you," she said. "Stay with us and keep on being the kindhearted boy you are."

Mrs. Lowry had an Irish smile and green eyes that could light up the dark side of the moon.

Chapter Eleven

THE SUN HAD set when I arrived at Jo Anne's house. The sky was the color of tin, striped with purple and black clouds. I thought perhaps she and I could be alone for the evening or go for ice cream in town. I couldn't have been more wrong. Henri Devos's Mustang was parked in the gravel driveway, and an old school bus was parked in the field, not far from the neighbor's hogpen. At least two lanterns were burning inside the bus. I knocked on Jo Anne's front door.

"Hi," she said upon opening it.

"Hi," I said.

Her hand didn't leave the doorknob. *"Hello?"* I said.

"Oh, come in."

I stepped inside and closed the door. She was wearing a flannel shirt and khaki pants without a belt. "I'm a little confused right now. We were going somewhere tonight?" she asked.

"Not necessarily. I just said I'd come by. Who are those people in the bus?"

"Some friends of Henri's."

"He's out there with them?"

"Yes."

"What are they doing here?"

"I'm not sure. Maybe they're beatniks. They're hardly more than children. Henri said they need a place to stay a few days. I'm a little overwhelmed right now."

"By what?"

"Maybe I made a mistake. It's not his fault."

"What are we talking about, Jo Anne?"

"I lent Henri five hundred dollars." She took a breath after she said it.

"Your professor asked you for five hundred dollars?"

"He said he'd pay me back in a few weeks. That was two months ago. I asked him if I could have it back, or at least part of it. He said his ex-wife put a lien on his car and bank account."

She sat down at the counter, one foot on the floor, the other tangled in a rung on the stool. She propped her forehead on the heel of her hand, her face in despair.

"There's more?" I said.

"He wants me to mortgage the house. He says he can double my money in a month. He says that's the only way he can make up the five hundred."

I looked out the window at the bus. I could see people inside, their silhouettes moving jerkily, like sticks, against the glow of the lanterns. I rubbed my eyes and looked again. This time they looked normal. "How is he going to double your money?"

"Buy into an art business in Dallas. He knows Bunker Hunt."

"Bunker Hunt the oilman?"

"Or whatever. He's a John Bircher." The top of her shirt was unbuttoned, her hair unbrushed. She pushed the loose button through its buttonhole with her thumb, hardly aware of what she was doing, the way people act when they have been betrayed or used or played for fools. I wanted to twist off Henri Devos's head and flush it down a commode.

"I'm sorry," she said. "I was about to take a shower. Then Henri drove up with his friends."

I looked through the window again. A black man had

opened the front door of the bus and stepped down gingerly in the weeds. He began urinating in a patch of yellow light.

"I need to have a conference with Henri," I said.

"Don't get into trouble, Aaron. I'll sit down with him later. He's not a bad person."

I went into the field. The temperature had dropped, and a mist was blowing coldly out of the north, and the grass was damp and swishing on the bottoms of my trousers. The urinating man zipped up and turned around, his mouth a circle of nicotine-stained teeth inside his long V-shaped beard, the kind a mountain man might wear. He was tall and wore strap overalls. His eyes went up and down my body. I was wearing a pair of Acme cowboy boots I had bought on Larimer Street in Denver. "Howdy," he said.

"Howdy," I said. "I'd like to see Mr. Devos if I could. Aaron Holland Broussard is the name."

"We're in the midst of a meditation right now."

"Could you demeditate? Just for a few seconds, so you can give him my message?"

"You may not know it, but you're in a holy place, man. The four cardinal points of the universe are pointed right at us."

"The place you just pissed on?"

He laid his hand on my shoulder. He breathed through his mouth, the whiskers around his lips moving. His breath was bilious, like a living presence on my skin. "I'm Marvin," he said.

I tried to step back. He tightened his hand on my shoulder and worked each finger deep into the muscle. I was surprised at his strength. "Do you fear your brother?" he asked.

I raised both my hands, forcing his grip from my shoulder. "Let me talk to Henri, then I'll be gone."

His eyes were lidless and contained a flickering fever-lit level of darkness and malevolence that a reasonable person does not try to plumb. "Wait here, Dixie Cup." He stuck his head inside the door. "Henri, got a cat here who talks hush puppy and seems to know you."

I tried to brush past him and get on the stairwell. "Hey!" he said.

"What?"

"I just said 'Hey,' as in 'Hey, mothafucker.' You got a race thing, 'cause I got a sense you think your shit don't stink."

His breath and spittle hit the side of my face. The combination was horrible. I wiped it off on my shoulder. "What are you talking about?"

"Don't look so serious, man. We're getting it on later. Dig? You're invited. The whole rainbow is in there." He stepped closer and lowered his voice. "Ten bucks, man. I'll give you any combo in there you want."

"Let me get by," I said. "Please."

His eyes were as shiny as obsidian, his teeth slanted sideways. A smile broke at the corner of his mouth. "Had you going, mothafucker. Ain't nobody gonna hurt those girls, man. What you're watching is a movement, I mean like a tidal wave. You hearing me, bubba? Shake hands. I won't hurt you. Stars and Bars forever."

He let me pass, then began laughing and couldn't stop until his knees were weak and he was forced to bend over and spit a wad of phlegm on the ground.

THE SEATS IN the bus had been ripped out and replaced with scarred furniture and stained mattresses and improvised hammocks and wash lines and paper bags soaked through with garbage and a gutted refrigerator bleeding rust from the door and a poster on the ceiling that showed Jesus smoking a joint.

Plastic inhalers were crushed and scattered on the floor. Henri Devos was stretched back in a reclining sun chair, one stamped with the green-and-white logo of Holiday Inn, his left arm crooked behind his neck. "Ah, the unpublished novelist from the mists of Avalon," he said to me. "I hope you brought your guitar."

Three girls and a boy were sitting on mattresses by his feet. One look at them and you knew their background. They were the detritus of a Puritan culture, one that made mincemeat of its children and left them marked from head to foot with every violation of the body that can be imposed on a human being: state homes, sexual molestation, sodomy, gang bangs, reformatory tats, fundamentalist churches, Venice Beach, Haight-Ashbury, maybe a porn gig in Vegas, maybe witness to a homicide in a boxcar or hobo jungle. Their hallmark was the solemnity, anger, and pain in their eyes.

"How about we toggle outside and check out the cardinal points of the universe?" I said to Henri.

"Another time," he said. "Let me introduce my friends." He repositioned himself but left his hand behind his neck and didn't bother to sit up as he pointed to the kids one by one.

Stoney had pipe-cleaner arms and jug ears and mindless blue eyes and hair the color and density of cotton candy. Moon Child wore Moe Howard bangs and a T-shirt that had been washed into cheesecloth and showed her nipples. Orchid could have been part black and part Indian or maybe part Asian, and had long clean hair streaked with purple and green dye and a white scar like a piece of string that ran through one eyebrow and caused one eyelid to droop. Lindsey Lou wore pigtails and a cowboy shirt and had the slimness of a barrel-racing rodeo girl and rings on all her fingers and jeans that looked painted on her legs.

"Pleased to meet y'all," I said.

"Wow, far out. I like the way you talk, man," Stoney said. "I've been down south myself, man. That way of talking is cool shit, man. It's definitely got musical qualities." His eyes had an ethereal glow, the pupils little more than fly specks.

"You here to fuck?" Moon Child said.

"I hadn't planned on it," I replied.

"Whoa, you guys," Henri said. "Our friend Aaron doesn't know when we're kidding."

"Then why is he here?" Moon Child said.

"He's a flatlander," Orchid said. "Visiting the zoo."

"You got a guitar?" Lindsey Lou said.

"I own a Gibson acoustic. But I didn't bring it."

"Far out," Stoney said.

"What kind of music do you play?" Lindsey Lou asked.

"Bluegrass and country, Woody Guthrie and Cisco Houston stuff."

"You mean the Cisco Kid, the guy who rides around with that fat slob who's always saying 'Let's went, Cisco'?" she said.

I saw Moon Child push a bong under a chair with her foot. "I didn't mean to break in on your meditation," I said.

"If you're not here to fuck or meditate," Moon Child said, "why are you here?"

"I dropped by to take Miss Jo Anne for some ice cream."

The boy and three girls stared at me as though looking at a memory they couldn't quite recall. Henri brushed a fly out of his face. Orchid reached into a small Indian-beaded drawstring purse and took out a joint and put it between her lips. "Ice cream?"

"Yeah, Trinidad has a great ice cream store," I said.

"Fucking far out, man," Stoney said.

Orchid half grinned at me, then lit the joint, the rings on her fingers a tangle of color under a lantern that hung from the ceiling. She took a deep hit and offered the joint to me with a lascivious wink. "We share everything."

"Thanks, I can't handle it," I said. "Same with alcohol."

"He's a narc," Moon Child said. "Ask him."

"Are you a narc?" Orchid said.

"I'm a migrant. From the San Joaquin down to the Rio Grande and everywhere in between."

"That's heavy, man," Stoney said. "Like a poem. I mean like 'The Star-Spangled Banner' or some shit."

"Y'all want to go for a walk?" I said. "We can knock on Jo Anne's door and pile into my car and get us some chocolate sundaes. My treat."

"What do you say, Henri?" Lindsey Lou asked.

"I'll have to pass," he said. He slapped at the worrisome fly again.

Lindsey Lou looked at me. "Sorry, Kemo Sabe."

"Because the professor doesn't want to go?" I said.

The kids dropped their eyes. Henri grinned at me. "Maybe another time, Natty."

"Natty?"

"Natty Bumppo," he said. "Braving the frontier, descending among the savages, showing us the way. I did a little research on you, pal. A friend of mine was a colleague of yours at your last teaching job."

"What'd you find?"

"You're a drunk. Know what a drunk is? A titty baby. Always looking for the nipple. Read Freud on the subject."

"I have," I said. "He nailed it, cocaine addict that he was."

"You were hired because your grandfather was hot shit in Louisiana."

"That's probably true." I reached down in my pocket and

opened the main blade on my Swiss Army knife. I sharpened it every three days. The blade could cut a stiff piece of paper as cleanly as a barber's razor.

"What are you doing?" he said.

"Not much. Natty Bumppo–type stuff."

He took his arm from behind his head and started to get up.

"I'd stay where you are," I said.

"Hey, fellow," Lindsey Lou said. "Yeah, you! Look at me. Cut this shit out. This is our home."

Orchid was getting to her feet. "She's right. Come on, man. You want to take a drive? That's cool. Hey, Marvin, Mayday in here! Stop playing pocket pool!"

"I told you he was a do-gooder," Moon Child said. "One with a twenty-four-hour hard-on."

I sawed the lantern loose from the ceiling. It was a Coleman, heavy in my hand, loaded with fuel. I unscrewed the cap on the base and poured kerosene oil all over Henri's head.

Stoney was crying and picking at his clothes as though they were filled with insects. "Don't do that! That's bad, and I mean really bad and not made-up bad, and the kind of shit crazy people do! What the fuck? What the fuck? What the fuck?" His needle was stuck, his face terrified. He hammered his feet up and down on the floor; his hands flailed in the air.

I shoved the lantern into Henri's hands, the wick still burning. "Early merry Christmas, you bastard," I said. "Pay Jo Anne the money you owe, or I'll rip out your spokes."

"What are you guys doing in here?" Marvin said behind me. He held a splintered board in his hand, a nail in the tip.

I pushed him backward off the bus, into the dark, then stepped down with him and pushed him again. He stumbled and righted himself, his mouth agape. The hogs were grunting and snuffing in the pen. A star dropped across the sky and disappeared behind a blue-black butte shaped like a chimney. "Lay off my threads, man," he said.

"You want to take the professor's fall?"

He dropped the board. It made a *thunk* when it hit the ground. He raised his palms so the light from Jo Anne's house would reflect on them. "I got no beef, chief."

"A big ten-four on that."

I started toward Jo Anne's house.

"Hey, man, I'm conwise and know where you got your rebop," he said at my back. "The pay is rotten when you pick state cotton. You been on the hard road, Joad. Way to go, Moe. We got your back, Jack. I didn't mean you no pain, Wayne."

"Thanks," I said. "I'll keep that in mind."

Alcohol and drug-induced psychosis can come in many ways. I suspected Marvin had tried them all.

Chapter Twelve

THE NEXT DAY I replaced the previous foreman, who had retired after thirty years of working for Mr. Lowry. Three weeks passed, and I got up each morning with a feeling that something good was going to happen that day, the way you feel when you're a kid and every day is an adventure. Mr. and Mrs. Lowry were fine people to work for. I had the run of the farm; the sky was blue from one horizon to the other, the days cool, the cottonwoods gold and green and shredding in the wind. Twice Mr. and Mrs. Lowry invited Jo Anne and me to supper. Something else was happening also. I was falling deeply in love with Jo Anne McDuffy. I had known only one other girl like her, the Jewish girl I had loved in high school, the girl with whom I had lost my virginity. Her name was Valerie Epstein. I loved Valerie with my heart and body and soul and would have given my life for her without a moment's hesitation because I believed she already owned it.

How did I lose such a wonderful young girl? Easy answer. It comes in bottles. The Broussard family had the patent on its destructive elements.

On a Saturday I took Jo Anne up the Gunnison River, and inside a pinkish-gray canyon I taught her how to fly-fish. After hooking herself once in the neck, she was out on a table rock in the middle of a riffle, lifting an elk-hair caddis fly from the surface, looping it lazily in a figure-eight pattern above her head, and letting it settle as naturally as a leaf between the riffle and the froth of a beaver dam. She was wearing tight khaki shorts and tennis shoes rather than waders, and her long legs were sunbrowned and shiny from the spray of the current sluicing over the rock. She caught a fourteen-inch rainbow and brought it in without a net, then squatted down to unhook it.

"If you're going to turn it loose, dip your hand first so you don't give it a fungus," I called.

She smiled and shook her head. It was obvious she couldn't hear because of the echo of the river inside the canyon walls. She wet her hand and cupped the rainbow's stomach and eased it back in the current, then dried her hands on her shorts and walked across the rock and stepped up on a fallen cottonwood, balancing with her arms, the rod flopping in one hand, until she was back on the bank.

"Wow!" she said.

"Where'd you learn to wet your hand before returning a fish to the stream?"

"Saw it on television."

"I brought some ham-and-onion sandwiches. You want to eat?"

"I want to fish some more."

The sun had slipped over the mountain, and a shadow had fallen on the bottom of the canyon wall, draining the glare from the water, turning it slate green. "It's about to get cold," I said.

"I don't care."

"You're something else," I said.

"In what way?"

"In every way."

I took the fly rod from her and leaned it against a willow

that had turned yellow with the season. I slipped my arms around her and pulled her against me and buried my face in her hair, then kissed her where her shoulder met her neck. I ached all over with desire when she stepped on my shoes and pressed her stomach against mine, her mouth parting.

"Oh, Jo Anne," I said.

"What?"

"I was just saying your name. Jo Anne McDuffy. What a grand Irish name."

She rubbed her face on my chest and squeezed me as hard as she could, not letting go, her tongue on my skin, her eyes closed, gripping me tighter and tighter until I thought my heart would burst.

I WANTED TO BELIEVE that somehow my troubles with the Vickers family and the iniquitous mindset they represented would go away, as well as the problem Henri Devos had created by arguably stealing what was at that time a large amount of money from a twenty-year-old girl who lived on tips. When I thought about that, I wanted to break my fists on his face.

On the Monday after Jo Anne and I had gone fishing, I asked Mr. Lowry for the afternoon off, with a promise to make it up on the weekend, and drove to the liberal arts building on the campus where Henri taught. He wasn't hard to find. Three female students were hanging in his office door while he was telling a joke, his feet on the desk. Then he bent his head sideways and looked at me through a space between their bodies. "Excuse me, ladies, an outlier friend of mine has just arrived," he said.

They laughed as they left, smiling at me, innocent to the core. I took off my hat and waved goodbye to them. Henri removed his feet from the desk and straightened his back. "Come in and close the door, please," he said.

"I think I'll leave it open. Jo Anne isn't the only one, is she?"

"You're mistaken, as always, Mr. Broussard."

"Forget the formality, you damn fraud. Where's the money you owe her?"

He lowered his eyes. "Would you close the door, please?"

"No."

His face soured. He bit on a thumbnail, then got up and closed the door and sat back down. "I'm working on repaying the debt. I've made some bad financial choices. I'm doing my best."

"Sell your Mustang."

"The loan company owns it."

"Take it to a bar and sell it anyway."

"I think I'm beginning to understand why you're no longer an educator."

"Where are the people in the bus?"

"Search me."

"Jo Anne says they ran an electrical cord to her house. The pig farmer says they took one of his hogs."

"I wouldn't know."

"Jo Anne did nothing to deserve these kinds of problems. What the hell is wrong with you?"

"Want me to call security?" he said.

"That might be a good idea."

"Stay away from me," he said, pushing his chair backward.

"Want to make a call? I'll help you."

I picked up the phone receiver from his desk and twisted the cord around his neck and tightened it until the blood to his brain shut down. Then I dumped the plastic wastebasket on his head and hammered it over his shoulders and flipped his chair over backward and jumped up and down on the basket. He looked like the top half of a refrigerator on the floor.

"Pay the money you owe Jo Anne, or I'm going to put your organs up for sale," I said. "Clank your head if you understand."

He understood.

TWO CRUISERS AND Wade Benbow's unmarked car forced me to the curb before I could make the highway. The deputies got out of their vehicles and headed toward me, their hands resting on their weapons. Benbow raised one hand for them to stop and pointed into my face with the other. "Get out of the car, Broussard!" he said.

I lifted my hands. "I'm reaching for the handle. Okay?"

"I wouldn't waste a bullet shooting you." He ripped the door open and jerked me out on the asphalt, then threw me against the car. When I tried to turn around, he stiff-armed me between the shoulder blades. "You really piss me off."

"If you want to be a hump for a man like Henri Devos, that's your problem," I said.

"Spread your feet."

"Eat shit," I said.

He slapped the back of my head, then lowered his voice. "Do it, kid."

I half looked at him.

"Do it," he repeated.

"Yes, sir," I replied.

"I'm going to hook you up and put you in the back seat now. Are we on the same page?"

"Yes, sir."

He snipped the handcuffs on me and opened the back door,

then put one hand on my head and eased me onto the seat. "I got it from here," he said to the deputies.

They waved and drove away. Benbow got behind the wheel and started the engine.

"What's the deal?" I said.

"The deal is shut up."

"Where are we going?"

"To school."

"What?"

"I told you to shut up."

He drove into an old part of Trinidad and parked behind the pool hall where Spud may have punctured the tires of the inmate who had sold him the stolen transistor radio. The alleyway was lined with garbage cans and paved with old brick that was sunken in the middle; a greasy stream of water ran all the way to the street.

"This is the school?" I said.

He got out and opened the back door. "Let's go."

I stepped out on the bricks, my wrists still manacled behind me. He took out his handcuff key and unhooked me.

"Why'd you put on that show for the deputies?" I said.

"What do you think?"

"I don't know."

"Some of them are too close to the Vickers family," he said. "Plus, I run my own investigation. Got it?"

The alley was deep in shadow, cool and damp, the sun blazing out on the sidewalk. "There's the back door of the poolroom," he said. "Your friend could have come out here, seen the victim on the sidewalk, and followed her. Would you argue with that?"

"I don't believe Spud would do that."

"Cut the crap. Your friend is a whoremonger. The murdered

woman was a five-dollar working girl. In her forties. According to our witness, the probable killer stopped her at the entrance to the alley, then they walked toward the hotel on the next block."

"The witness identified Spud?"

"No, he didn't see the guy's face."

"Why are you telling me all this?"

He reached under the driver's seat of his car and opened a manila folder. It contained four black-and-white crime-scene photos, all of the same victim. They were worse than the ones he had shown me previously.

"Those are ice-pick holes?"

"Either that or something like it."

"Was she alive when he did that?"

"The coroner says probably."

"Jesus," I said. "Why her eyes?"

"Why do these guys do anything?"

He took the photos out of my hands. I felt dizzy. A rat ran from a garbage can and splashed across the water and disappeared under a pile of cardboard boxes.

"What are you thinking?" he asked.

"Nothing."

"Yeah, you are. This is where your friend could have gotten the box he used. He made a sling out of his bandana, put his arm in it, put the box under his other arm, then got her in an alley and put her through hell."

"I'll never believe Spud capable of doing something like that. No matter what you say."

"You're like most people. You got a big blind spot. You don't want to believe monsters live among us."

"Spud isn't a monster."

"Pull your head out of your ass. I know what Jude Lowry has told you."

"He hasn't told me anything."

"Don't lie. He told you I'm determined to prove my granddaughter was murdered by a serial killer because I can't admit I let her out of my sight. Did or did he not tell you that?"

"He didn't mean it in a bad way, Benbow."

"*Detective* Benbow."

"Yes, sir."

"There're people who look like the rest of us, but they feed on evil. Are they born like that? No one knows. They take their secrets to the grave. My own guess is they make a conscious choice to murder the light in their souls. They never come back from that moment."

"Are you going to take me in?" I asked.

"Over the beef with Devos? He won't file charges."

"How do you know that?"

"My wife works at the college. He's up for that lifetime job guarantee, you know, what do they call it?"

"Tenure?"

"Yeah, that's it," he said. "Tenure. Get in the passenger seat. I'll take you back to your car."

But there was something missing from our conversation, a detail that didn't fit in the behavior of the hooker and the man with the box under his arm.

"He knew her," I said.

"Who knew her?"

"The killer. Five-dollar hookers don't do good deeds in the wee hours for strangers on the street."

"Your bud Caudill probably came out of the womb with a hard-on. You don't think he fits the profile?"

"A john wouldn't have to deceive her. He'd just walk her down the street to a hotel or take her somewhere in his car."

"You're a smart kid," he said.

"I've got to get back to Mr. Lowry's farm, Detective."

"Remember when I told you I wanted to quit smoking?"

"You beat it?"

"I've got the big C. In both lungs. That means the wrong people better not mess with me. You're dragging a chain, Broussard. I don't know what it is, but don't screw up your life." He stuck his business card in my shirt pocket. "That's it. School's out. Latch your seat belt."

Chapter Thirteen

THAT EVENING JO Anne started a new job as a cook at a hamburger joint, and I spent the evening in the bunkhouse with my J-50 Gibson guitar. Much of the crew had headed for the Rio Grande Valley in Texas or southern New Mexico or Arizona. Spud Caudill and Cotton Williams had decided to stay on. Spud said he was innocent of any crime, and he didn't want to be charged after he'd left the state and get brought back as a fugitive and have flight used against him. Cotton said he was too old for the border and the culture of drugs and alcohol and diseased Mexican girls; he thought it was time for him to consider buying a poultry ranch or a truck farm.

I didn't quite believe either of them. Spud was infatuated with a barmaid in Walsenburg. As for Cotton, I couldn't forget his implied threat about putting six feet of dirt in the faces of the Vickers team. I also couldn't forget his story about wiping out a nest of SS deep in the Roman catacombs.

The bunkhouse was a long building, clean and well lighted, with a cubicle for the foreman, not unlike an army barracks. But when it was empty, it could be a very lonely place, and on this particular evening I felt memories of the past trying to catch up with me, like a specter trying to serve a summons or a figure dressed in leather honing a knife on a whetstone. I was also bothered by every aspect of my conversation with Wade

Benbow. Why had Mr. Lowry been so certain that Benbow's negligence was responsible for the death of the grandchild? Benbow was not a weak man. He was looking death in the face and seemingly without fear. Why would he spend his remaining time on earth chasing a serial killer who didn't exist?

Last, Benbow's mention of monsters in our midst would not go away. All my life I'd had the same feelings. I was raised to believe that redemption could occur as quickly as looking up suddenly at a burst of sunlight inside a raincloud and realizing you had just been set free from all the dark days that had beset you. If that were true, and I believed it was, how could some be born with the lights of pity and mercy already robbed from their eyes?

Even though I had witnessed the electrocution of a man in a southern prison, and seen individual acts of cruelty perpetrated on people of color for no reason other than to humiliate and degrade them, I did not understand that real evil was collective in nature until I heard the lyrics of two black convicts recorded in Angola by an academic named Harry Oster. That might seem strange, but as a southerner, I had listened too long to chivalric tales and the horns blowing along the road to Roncevaux rather than the leathery whistle of the razor strop called the Black Betty.

One of the singers, Robert "Guitar" Welch, sang a couplet I couldn't get out of my head: "Wonder why they electrocute a man twelve o'clock at night / The current much stronger, the people turn out all the light."

Another convict, Matthew "Hogman" Maxey, sang about the desperation of an inmate assigned to the Red Hat gang, a group who wore black-and-white stripes and straw hats painted red and were forced to run their wheelbarrows double-time up and down the levee from sunrise to sunset. Those who fell out were stretched on anthills or shot. Over one hundred bodies were buried in the levee, anonymous and forgotten, in summer their resting place a fairyland of green grass and buttercups, as though the earth wished to console them at least partially for their misfortune.

The lyric he sang? "I axed my captain, 'Captain, tell what's right.' / He whupped my left, then say, 'Boy, now you know what's right.'"

I sat down on the bed in my cubicle and made an E chord on my Gibson and ran my plectrum across the strings. The resonance of the old-time Gibson acoustic guitars had no peer. The bass strings rumbled like distant thunder; the treble strings tinkled like crystal. When you curved your fingers into the neck, the chord seemed to make itself, as though an angel were guiding your hand. I began to sing my favorite Jimmie Rodgers song, "Blue Yodel No. 1."

T for Texas, T for Tennessee,
T for Texas, T for Tennessee,
T for Thelma, the gal who made a fool out of me.

I felt a shadow move across my body and then my hands and guitar, and looked up into Cotton's face.

"Hey, what's happenin'?" I said.

"Thought you'd like to play some checkers."

"Sure," I said.

He unfolded the board on my bed, then opened a box of checkers and began placing them on the squares.

"What happened to your thumb?" I said.

"Hit it with a hammer."

"You want a soda?"

"I wouldn't mind."

I went to the machine at the end of the bunkhouse and came back with two cans. "That's a lot of tape."

"Looks like an M1 thumb," he said. "Know what that is?"

"You press the clip in the magazine with your thumb, then roll it out before the bolt snaps on it and fixes you up proper."

"You told me you weren't in the service."

"I read about it in a book."

His good eye lingered on me. I started to pop both soda cans, but he picked his up before I could, covering the top with his palm. "You go first," he said.

When I talked with Cotton, I always felt I was looking at half a face. "Are you planning on doing some payback?"

"On the Vickerses?"

"Who else would I be talking about?"

"That kid has been shooting off his mouth in a couple of bars."

"About what?"

"How he kicked our asses."

"Kids shoot off their mouths."

He smiled. "That's true. Come on, it's your move."

"You've been around the block, Cotton. You know better than to play on the other man's terms. I'm talking about messing with the Vickers family."

He glanced at my guitar case, open on the bed. "The skillet shouldn't be lecturing to the kettle." The lid to the compartment in the guitar case where I normally kept my picks and strings and a capo was open. Cotton flipped the lid shut. "Mr. Lowry know you have that?"

"I don't remember it coming up in our conversation."

"You don't have no business with a gun."

"Wonder why the Second Amendment is in the Bill of Rights."

He knitted his fingers, then unknitted and knitted them again. He began placing the checkers back in the box, softly, one at a time. "I'm more tired than I thought. Age sneaks up on you."

"Don't get your thumb infected."

He fitted the top on the checker box. "I don't like people being untruthful to me, Aaron."

"Untruthful about what?"

"Locking and loading and firing an M1 when you're about to brown your britches."

"I've got six years in my life that are like Swiss cheese, Cotton. I'm lucky I can tie my shoes."

THE NEXT EVENING I drove to the hamburger joint where Jo Anne was working. I couldn't believe what I saw. Like a traveling Visigoth culture that had found a wormhole in the dimension, the people who lived in the school bus were parked behind the Dumpster in back. Through the windows, I could see the whole crew: Stoney and Moon Child and Orchid and Lindsey Lou and Marvin, all of them eating out of Styrofoam containers. I parked on the street, under a row of maple trees, and approached the bus from the back, then stepped into the vestibule.

The girls looked at me blankly. Marvin wore a wilted black cowboy hat that shadowed the top half of his face, his mouth full of food, his whiskers slick with grease and matted with crumbs. Only Stoney showed any reaction. His face lit up like a pink light bulb. "Hey, it's you! The ice cream guy! Hey, you guys! It's him! Come on, ice cream guy, sit down!"

"Mind if I have a word with you all?" I said.

"We've been looking for you, man," Marvin said, tapping the air. "We met this guy, see, he's a prophet. I mean he's been *sent*, you dig? I'm talking about illumination, man, on the first day of creation. I'm talking about a burst of light rippling across the fucking universe."

"I'd like to talk with y'all about running up Jo Anne's electric bill," I said. "The neighbor is a little upset about one of his hogs, too."

"We didn't steal anybody's hog," Marvin said.

"I didn't say you did."

"Hogs don't commit suicide. So if the hog didn't commit suicide, it must be missing. That means you're talking about stealing. So, *yeah*, you did accuse us of stealing. That's hurtful, man."

"Don't talk to him," Moon Child said to him. Her eyes were black and swimming with hostility.

"I think y'all are good people," I said.

"What's that supposed to mean?" she said.

"Henri Devos is not good people," I said. "He's a con man. If he's around other people, it's for reasons of money, sex, or control."

"Guy's an artist, maybe a little over the line, but mellow most of the time," Marvin said. "We heard about you going apeshit in his office. You need to dial your head down a little bit, use restraint, not cram a telephone pole up your own ass. It ain't smart."

"He took Jo Anne for five hundred dollars. That's why I'm asking y'all not to hurt her any more than she's been hurt."

"*Fuck* you. We don't hurt anybody," Moon Child said.

As I looked at Moon Child, with her round pie-plate face and cavernous eyes, and at Orchid, with her clean purple and green hair, and Lindsey Lou, the rodeo girl with pigtails and western shirt and figure like a whip, I wondered if they dreamed of an ancient stone bowl that contained magical properties, perhaps carved from the rock in a Judaic mountain and brimming with water that had been snow only yesterday, a balm that rinsed away the injustice done the innocent and made all things new. The bruises on their souls hovered in their eyes, and

I was sure that each of them shared a commonality they would pay any cost to forget. The commonality I mean was the moment the father figure in the home placed his hand on top of his daughter's head and looked into her eyes and said, *Be gone from my sight.*

But if my speculation was correct, I did not want to show it. "Can y'all give Jo Anne a break?"

"We like her," Lindsey Lou said. "She's a sister."

"See, we own nothing," Orchid said. Her drooping eyelid gave the affect of someone aiming down a rifle barrel. "By owning nothing, we're allowed to share in everything. One day we're going to a tropical place where the people eat the fruit from the trees and the fish from the sea and nothing else. They don't die, either."

"Who taught you this?" I said.

"Ours to know," she said. "Why don't you and Jo Anne join us?"

"I have to make a living," I said.

"Poor you," she said. She pursed her lips. "We share everything."

"I see," I said.

"You don't see anything," Moon Child said. "And here's something else for you to chew on, asshole. What we do is none of your fucking business."

"Don't be hard on him, Moon Child," Lindsey Lou said. "We've been living off his girlfriend." She looked at me. "Did you see the holy man who just left?"

"Holy man?" I said. "No, I don't think I did. Does he glow with blue fire?"

"We're talking about Bible-thumping Bob," Marvin said.

I was starting to lose attention.

"His face got fried, so he wears a veil or a black hood," Marvin said. "Depending on the venue."

"Nice seeing y'all," I said.

"There's more," Marvin said. "The hood doesn't have eye-holes in it."

The girls were smiling now.

"Y'all taking me over the hurdles?" I said.

"No. Hang around," Orchid said. "We'll introduce you."

"Hey, ice cream guy," Stoney said, suddenly erect, as though someone had just clicked a switch on his back. "Stay away from . . . stay away from . . . stay away from . . . " He couldn't finish the sentence. He started twitching, pulling at his shirt as he had done before. Then he wept. The girls put their hands on him.

"What's wrong, partner?" I said. "What should I stay away from?"

"Don't go near the hills. Where all those miners and children and women got killed."

I couldn't take it any longer. The drug culture had just commenced its long slog across the country, but I was convinced these kids had already dipped their brains in hallucinogens and probably would never undo the damage. I left the bus and went into the hamburger joint. I could see Jo Anne in the kitchen, cooking a wire basket full of french fries, her face bright with sweat, her eyes watering in the smoke. She wiped her eyes on her forearm and blew me a kiss.

I wanted to lift her on my shoulder and pack her over the mountains into a place where neither moth nor rust doth corrupt and where men do not break through and steal, maybe the same imaginary kingdom a sad kid like Orchid had described, a haven I had just derided, silently, perhaps, but derided just the same.

Chapter Fourteen

DURING HER BREAK, Jo Anne and I had some ice cream in a booth in back. "Ever hear of a holy man named Bible-thumping Bob?" I asked. "A fellow who wears a black hood with no eyeholes?"

"You're serious?" she said.

"Our friends in the bus say he was hanging around when God created light."

She was cleaning out the bottom of her paper cup with a spoon. "Local?" she said without looking up.

"I forgot to ask."

"When did you see the bus crowd?"

"Just a while ago. They weren't in here?"

"I think I would have noticed."

"They were parked by the Dumpster in back," I said.

"Yuck."

"I asked them to leave us alone," I said. "They're not bad kids. Maybe Marvin is a bad fellow, but the kids aren't."

"What makes Marvin so bad?"

"Maybe that's too strong. He threatened me with a board that had a nail in it, but he backed down. He's probably a pimp and a small-time thief and paperhanger. He's not what you call mainline."

"What's 'mainline'?"

"A recidivist or psychopath. The kind of fellow other convicts walk around."

"How do you know all this?"

"I'm just saying most people don't get to choose who they are. It's a lesson I've never learned very well."

She set her feet on top of mine and tapped them up and down, her eyes bright, her fingers twined in mine. Then she looked toward the entrance, and the light went out of her face. "Don't turn around. Darrel Vickers and his father just came in."

"Why are all these people showing up this evening?" I said.

"Welcome to Trinidad on a weekday night."

I started to turn my head. She whacked my knuckles with her metal spoon. "Did you hear me?"

"That hurt."

"Start something with the Vickerses and see what I do later."

"What are they doing now?"

"Headed straight for us. I mean it, Aaron. Don't say one word to them."

"Why would I want to talk with the Vickers family?"

Her eyes went out of focus.

Then both the father and son were standing inches from us, Rueben Vickers wearing a smile that was like lipstick painted on a lopsided muskmelon, Darrel fresh-shaved and in a Confederate kepi and a lavender T-shirt scissored off beneath the nipples, his love handles peeking out from his beltless jeans, his coppery hair thick with grease and combed back in ducktails. He rotated his head as though he had a crick in his neck, his eyes rolling around the room.

Mr. Vickers fitted his hand like a clothespin on my shoulder. "How you doin', boy?" he said.

I looked straight ahead. A fat, sweaty man with tats wrapped around both arms was scraping a stove with a spatula. He wiped his face on his shoulder, simultaneously smelling himself.

Mr. Vickers kneaded my collarbone, his nails dipping into the muscle. "Sorry about what happened at Jude's place," he said. "I get my quills up sometimes."

"Forget it," I said.

"Listen to this kid," he said. "You got moxie, boy."

"Not me," I said.

"Does this kid have moxie or not?" Vickers said to his son.

"Yes, Daddy, he has," Darrel said.

"See?" Mr. Vickers said. "I know when a boy's got sand and when he doesn't." He grinned at Jo Anne. "How you doin' tonight, little lady?"

"I'm not little, thank you," she said. "Unless you mean my social status. Is that what you mean, Mr. Vickers? I belong to a lower social class?"

He coughed out a laugh. "Hey, what's goin' on here? I stopped by to be nice."

"We're all right here, Mr. Vickers," I said.

"Yeah?" he said. "Then that's good. The way to be. When a guy is having some ice cream with his lady. Isn't that right, Darrel?"

"Yes, sir," Darrel said.

"I think my boy might want to manage one of these. What do you say, Darrel?"

"Let's order, Daddy."

"What's tasty in here, hon?" Mr. Vickers said to Jo Anne. "I mean finger-lickin' good."

"You've never been here before?" she said.

His face was licentious, like soft candy melting in front of a candle. "You're smart. You know how to handle yourself. I like that. I like that uniform, too. The way it fits."

"Why'd you hurt Aaron?" she said.

I touched the top of her hand. "It's all right, Jo."

"Aaron did nothing to you or your son, Mr. Vickers," she said. "You beat him with a horsewhip. In the face."

"I just told you I was sorry for that. I got a temper. What am I supposed to do?"

"We're done, sir," I said.

"Fine with me." But he didn't take his hand from my shoulder. In fact, he drummed his fingers on it. "I got a favor to ask you. You said I had a demon in me. An incubus or some stuff like that."

"Daddy, don't get into it," Darrel said.

"What made you say a thing like that?" Mr. Vickers asked me.

"You're cruel when you don't have to be," I said.

His tongue slid along his lips. "What do you mean when I don't *have* to be? What kind of talk is that?"

"You're pathological," I said. "It's not your fault."

Mr. Vickers looked at his son. "What's he talking about?"

"He gets it from *her*," Darrel said. "She learned some intellectual words at the juco. She's the cause of all of this. She made up those lies about us and called the cops."

"You told Darrel I served the Prince of Darkness?" Mr. Vickers said.

"You just got eighty-sixed, Mr. Vickers," Jo Anne said.

"I'm eighty-sixed from a teenage dump? How bad does it get?"

"It's not funny, Daddy," Darrel said.

"Quiet," Mr. Vickers said. "I'm the one getting barbecued."

"Take yourself and your father out of here, Darrel," Jo Anne said.

Darrel's eyes were the rheumy blue of marbles you might see in the murk at the bottom of an aquarium. They slipped across Jo Anne's face and hair and throat and breasts, then lighted on her mouth. "Bitch," he said.

"Hey! None of that!" Mr. Vickers said. He pointed at Jo Anne and me. "Soon as you close, we'll go for a drink."

"Where?" she said.

I couldn't believe she would entertain the idea.

"A new club downtown," he said. "Strictly class, no riffraff. They got good food."

"Wait here."

"No, we're not going to do this, Mr. Vickers," I said.

"Listen up," he said. "We either settle this now, or I'll give you a boxing lesson you won't forget. With one hand, kid. In public."

I heard a loud rattling and rumbling sound, like metal wheels grinding heavily on a hard surface. Jo Anne rounded a counter dragging a huge bucket sloshing with a foamy aggregate of gray water, Ajax, kitchen grease, liquid floor wax, Lysol, dirt, and the swab-out from the toilet bowls and urinals. The long, thick strings of the mop looked like clumps of dead eels among the bubbles.

She swung the mop across Mr. Vickers's face, the strings wrapping around his head, saturating his face and chest, showering the next booth. He fell backward, landing on his spine, a piece of mop string curled on his cheek. She turned in a circle and swung with both hands and bounced Darrel off a table that was bolted to the floor. Before he could get up, she plunged the mop into the bucket and whipped it down on his head. The floor was sopping. Both father and son were gagging and spitting water and string, both slipping and struggling to stand, like drunk ice skaters. A little girl with her mother pointed and said, "Look, Mommy, funny men fall down." A police car that had been passing by made a U-turn, its flasher on, its siren off.

Jo Anne prodded the Vickerses out the door, into the night, jabbing them in the face each time they tried to speak.

"The Golden Arches have nothing on us," she said. "Come back anytime. Bring the whole family."

God, I loved Jo Anne McDuffy.

Chapter Fifteen

THAT NIGHT THERE was dry thunder in the hills, then lightning split the sky and hailstones came down like shrapnel on a tin roof. Nonetheless, I fell into a deep sleep and dreamed of a place where I did not want to go. In the dream, the moon was down, the hills dark humps in the distance, the night still except for the wind and the Chinese blowing their bugles behind their lines. A command post was perched at the top of the grade above a meandering ditch piled with sandbags and reinforced by telegraph poles that had been sawed down by a railway track and dragged to the firing line. Far down the slope, trip flares popped in the sky, then swung inside their own heat and incandescence above a moonscape that contained not one blade of grass or cup of potable water, a piece of hell that contained no living thing other than the organisms dissolving the dead half-buried in shell holes.

Two soldiers were running through a byzantine network of trenches up the hillside, trying to get back to their lines from a listening post that a Chinese probe had stumbled on. Covering fire full of tracer round streamed over their heads. Then flamethrowers captured by the Chinese burst alight and arched over the trenches, filling the air with a smell like carbon monoxide and a whooshing sound, followed by a secondary sound like the mewing of a kitten.

In my sleep, I tried to fight my way out of the dream. I felt I was encased in mud or wet cement. I wanted to fill my head with alcohol or opiates or pornographic images to prevent what I was about to witness. The ground was shaking from the 105 rounds bursting on the hillsides to the north, then someone screwed up and an artillery round came in short and slammed me to the earth, ripping the breath from my lungs. My rifle flew from my hands. My steel pot scissored down on the bridge of my nose. My nostrils and mouth were clogged with dirt that stank of cordite. I knew I was about to die.

"Wake up," a voice was saying.

"Medic!" I heard myself say.

"You're having a dream," the voice said. A hand shook my shoulder, then shook it harder. "It's Cotton. You got the screaming meemies."

"Where am I?"

"In the bunkhouse. Who's Saber?"

"My best friend."

"Some guy who bought it?"

"I don't know."

"You should go to the VA, Aaron."

My eyes were fully open now. Cotton was sitting on the side of my bunk.

"I wasn't in the army," I said. I sat up and pressed the heels of my hands against my temples. "I just have to clean out my head. I've had nightmares all my life. Don't pay attention to me."

"I took this from under your pillow," he said. "You were try-ing to get your hand on it."

He flipped open the cylinder of the .38 snub nose and dumped the rounds from the chambers and tilted them out of his palm onto the nightstand. "In a war, we all do things we're ashamed of," he said. "You don't have the copyright on that."

I went into the latrine and fell on my knees in front of a commode and retched for almost five minutes.

THE DAWN WAS gray and misty, the pastures wet and lime green, the hills barely visible. I got up before anyone else and walked down to the dining hall. Through the window, I could see Chen Jen, our Chinese cook, stirring pancake batter in a big bowl. I walked past the dining hall and down to the small wood bridge over the creek and through the cottonwoods into the fog.

I heard elk *glunk*ing, then I saw their antlers and the steam rising from their backs and the brightness in their eyes. Maybe they had been bugling. It was that time of year. Perhaps their bugling was the origin of my dream, I told myself. Maybe I was not the driven man who feared his nocturnal thoughts or who, in the middle of the day, could step sideways through an invisible door just the other side of his fingertips and not come back for hours.

I kept walking toward the elk, then realized I was not alone. A figure shrouded with fog was standing stock-still ten yards from me. "Spud?" I said.

"It's me," he replied. He was wearing bib overalls and rubber boots and his fedora. He had a tree branch in his hand.

"What are you doing?" I asked.

"There were some hunters up there on the hill. That's Lowry property."

"The season's not open."

"They start nosing around early."

"You talked with the hunters?"

"You might call it that."

"You got in their face?"

"I told them to get their sorry asses down the road before I went upside somebody's head."

I tried to see through the fog. An elk bugled, then I heard the clatter of their racks and the huffing sounds of combat and the thud of hooves and a sickening screech, as though one of them had been hooked in the eye. "Hunting doesn't set well with you?" I said.

"Shooting animals for sport is cruel. I hate those sons of bitches."

"What time did you get up?"

"About the time you were yelling in your sleep." He sailed the branch like a boomerang into the fog.

"You didn't take one of the vehicles into town and get your ashes hauled, did you?" I said.

"*What*, you think I'm in rut, like those elks out there?"

"I was just kidding," I lied. "Want to get some grub?"

We walked back to the dining hall, the grass streaking our trousers, the sun like a frail pink rose behind the mountains. The only other trail of broken grass in the field was the one I had made earlier.

WHETHER JO ANNE wanted me to or not, after ten that morning I called the hamburger joint to see if I could save her job. I was surprised to learn that she had not been fired. The owner told her the situation was not her fault and that he was proud of her. I was even more surprised that afternoon when Mr. Lowry came out to the barn where six of us were putting on a new roof. "You got a call, Aaron," he said. "You can get it in the dining hall."

"Do you know who it is?"

He walked away without answering. I climbed down the ladder and went into the dining hall. Chen Jen was mopping down the tables. "Mr. Lowry said I had a call," I said.

"Yes, you have call from stupid man who yell to show how stupid he is."

I went to the counter and picked up the receiver. "Hello?"

"That you, Broussard?"

"Who do you think it is, Mr. Vickers?"

"Pull your dork out of the lamp socket. I was out of line. I told the hamburger guy that."

"You called the owner of your own volition?"

"Of my own what?" he said.

"What do you want from me?"

There was a long silence.

"Are you still there?" I asked.

"Am I here? Are you retarded? Where would I go? Why do you think I called?"

"Sir, I have no idea."

"That's what I mean. You just said 'sir.' You got manners. When you got manners, you got a leg up on other people. I can't teach my boy that. I've got an IQ twenty points higher than Wernher von Braun, but I'm from Jerksville on manners."

"I've got a crew on our barn roof, Mr. Vickers. I had better get back to work."

"What I'm telling you is I'm a hothead. That doesn't mean I don't care about my son. I've done everything I could. I gave him the strop. That didn't work. I sent him to military school. He got thrown out. So what I'm telling you is watch out for that girl."

My ear felt dirty, as though someone had put spittle in it. "You're telling me Darrel plans to hurt Jo Anne?"

"I got no idea what's in his head. He fell off an electric hobby-horse when he was a little boy. *That's* what I'm saying."

"You need to talk to Detective Benbow."

"I call him *Bimbo*."

"You do him a disservice," I said.

"You walk around with a thesaurus? Where'd you learn to talk English? Protect your girl, but don't you hurt my boy. If you have trouble, you call me. Got a pencil?"

SUNDAY AFTERNOON JO Anne and I saw *Lonely Are the Brave* at a theater in Trinidad. It was written by Dalton Trumbo and Edward Abbey and starred Kirk Douglas and George Kennedy and Gena Rowlands. Douglas plays a cowboy named Jack Burns who cuts wire fences wherever he has the opportunity and punches out a cop in order to be jailed so he can free a friend who was imprisoned for aiding illegal immigrants. The friend is a family man and cannot risk a jailbreak, so Jack removes the hacksaw blades he has hidden inside the tops of his cowboy boots and cuts through the bars and escapes with two Indians. In the last scene, Jack tries to ride his horse across a highway into Mexico and is run over by a truck loaded with commodes, driven by Carroll O'Connor.

After the show, we walked toward a coffee shop. The neon lighting on the bars and restaurants was just coming on. The shadows were long in the street, the wind unseasonably cold. Jo Anne had said hardly a word since we left the theater.

"You okay?" I said.

"It's a dark film," she replied.

"Look at it this way. Jack Burns is the outsider who sets the standard for the rest of the cast. Even the sheriff, the Walter Matthau character, is actually on Jack's side."

"The good people of the world get it in the neck, and nobody cares," she said. "That's the message."

We went inside the coffee shop and ordered pie and coffee. I wished we hadn't seen the film.

"Is something wrong, Jo Anne?"

"Somebody broke out the back windows of my house. I also lost my scholarship at the juco."

"When were your windows broken?"

"Two nights ago."

"Why didn't you tell me?"

"I didn't want you to go after Darrel Vickers."

"Are you sure he did it?"

"Take it to the bank," she said.

"What happened with the scholarship?"

"Henri is my academic adviser. He told the dean my commitment and my attendance had become erratic and he couldn't recommend me any longer."

"I wish I had known."

"What would you have done? Beat him up again in his office?"

I remained silent while the waitress put down our coffee and pie. Outside, a woman was chasing her hat in the wind. On it was a long feather like a thin black quill. The feather went one way and the hat another. "I'm sorry, Jo Anne."

"Stop it. It's just the way things are." She gazed at the woman outside. "That poor lady. Somehow she makes me think of my father."

I really didn't want to hear it, but I said, "How so?"

"He believed nature was his friend," she said. "Then a cyclone pulled him into the sky. Sometimes I think he's still out there, wandering in his blindness."

Chapter Sixteen

At noon Monday Mr. Lowry came to the dining hall door and signaled to me at the table where Spud, Cotton, and Maisie were eating. I took my coffee with me. "Yes, sir?" I said.

"Wade Benbow wants you to call him," he said. He handed me a slip of paper with a telephone number on it. "He doesn't want it known he's contacting you."

"Has something happened to Jo Anne?"

"He just said he wanted to have a private talk with you."

"I'm sorry all this trouble keeps overflowing on your farm, Mr. Lowry."

"Maybe it's time to stay away from the wrong people, Aaron."

"Sir?"

"Trinidad is a small town. I heard about you knocking around that art professor. You think that achieved something?"

"He did serious injury to Jo Anne, Mr. Lowry."

"You made him the victim and yourself the villain. I'd call that a bad trade."

He walked away without saying goodbye. He had never corrected me before. My coffee cup felt like lead in my hand.

At quitting time, I called the number Wade Benbow had given Mr. Lowry.

"Hello?" Benbow said.

"You wanted to talk to me, Detective?"

"I need your help. I'd like for you to come out to my house. Now."

"I was fixing to drop by Jo Anne's workplace."

"What's stopping you from doing both?"

His metal-roofed log house was high up on a hill and deep in the woods above the opening to Ratón Pass. Down below I could see a motel, its neon lights already on, and to the north the sloping brick streets of Trinidad and the glimmering of the sun's reflection on the magical razor-blue mountain that rose like a tombstone above the city.

Benbow stood on the porch, wearing a beat-up bomber jacket, half-top boots, and a slouch hat, a revolver tucked inside his belt. A can of beer was balanced on the porch rail. In back a pickup truck was parked in a paintless, ancient garage so narrow in its construction it resembled a coffin.

"Want a beer?"

"No, sir," I said.

"Come in back. Let's see what kind of shot you are."

"What's this about, Detective?"

"Call me Wade." He stepped down from the porch with his can of beer and began walking around the side of the house. "Coming?"

"I have to leave in the next fifteen minutes."

"What's the urgent situation in fifteen minutes?"

"I'll think of something," I replied.

The backyard was sliced with the shadows of pine trees, a cold wind puffing out of a dry creek bed that threaded through an arroyo behind the house. I thought I saw a mountain lion jump across the rocks in the creek bed and clamber uphill through the tree trunks.

"Is that what I think it is?" I asked.

"They come down sometimes. They think this country is still theirs. There're things up on that hill that are worse than cougars, though."

"Like what?"

"This was the northern tip of a Comanche empire. They did things with fire it's better not to think about. I can show you tipi rings and the remains of human bones up there, some of them children's."

"I don't want to hear about it, Detective."

"Wade." He pulled the revolver from his belt. It was a .357 Magnum snub. "See that bucket on the post about twenty feet up the creek? Think you can punch a hole or two in it?"

"Expensive ammunition for target practice."

He handed me a pair of earplugs wrapped in cellophane. "Since I contracted the big C, I find myself less inclined to worry about the cost of bullets."

I aimed with both hands, my feet slightly spread, and fired six times before I lowered the weapon. I pulled the plug from one ear.

He took a sip of his beer. "You learn to shoot at Braille school?"

I looked back at the bucket.

"I'm joking," he said. "You're heck on wheels, Broussard."

"Why are you doing this, Detective?"

"Wade."

"Sorry, I was raised to address my elders in only one fashion."

"I know the pawnshop owner who sold you the thirty-eight. I hope you're not entertaining cowboy fantasies."

"I gave up being other people's litter box."

"I was afraid you'd say something like that. Let's sit down a minute."

He eased himself down on a back step and looked blankly into the woods. Some might call his eyes dead. But for something to die, it must first be alive, and I saw no sign of loss or anger or remorse or even injury in his face, as though I were looking at a prosthesis rather than tissue. The lack of expression in Detective Benbow was the kind you see in people who have witnessed events that forever change their view of the world. They never talk about it or struggle with it. Instead, they accept the fact that human beings are capable of deeds Satan couldn't think up.

"Mr. Benbow?" I said.

"What?"

"Were you in the war?"

"Yeah. Why do you ask?"

"I just wondered."

He shook it off. "Yesterday the body of another woman was found way back in some rocks down the Pass. The body might have been there several days. Cause of death, broken neck. She could have fallen from a cliff. Or somebody could have dragged her there. She was a hooker." He held his eyes on mine.

"Okay?" I said.

"Got any reason to believe your friend Spud Caudill might have been involved?"

I tried to keep my face empty and not to swallow. In my mind's eye, I saw Spud in the fog and heard the bugling of the elk and his claim that he was up early driving off poachers.

"Well?" Benbow said.

"Why pick on poor Spud?"

"Because he frequents the cathouse where the hooker worked on and off."

"I have nothing to say about Spud, sir."

"How about Marvin Fogel, the driver of the four-wheel zoo?"

"I think he's a junkie and a meltdown." I studied my watch and avoided his eyes.

"Meaning?"

"I had a misunderstanding with him. He was carrying a splintered board, one with a sixteen-penny nail in it."

"One that could make a wound like an ice pick?"

"That's possible."

"And you decided to keep this information to yourself?"

"You know why jails are filled with pitiful people?"

"Tell me," he said.

"They're easy to catch."

He stood up and flicked the last drops of his beer into the flower bed, then dropped the can in a trash bag swollen with more cans. "Actually, I made us a couple of sandwiches."

"I promised to eat with Jo Anne."

He wiped his nose with the back of his wrist. "You asked me about my service time. I was with the 103rd, the Cactus Division. We liberated a subcamp of Dachau. It was quite a place."

"I appreciate the invitation, Detective Benbow."

"Wade," he replied.

FRIDAY NIGHT THE United Farm Workers of America sponsored a candlelight service at the site of the Ludlow Massacre. Jo Anne and I went, and so did Spud, Cotton, Maisie, Mr. and Mrs. Lowry, and most of the crew who hadn't drug up (as it was called) and headed for the Rio Grande Valley. There must have been at least two hundred people gathered by the horizontal metal door and the steps that led down to the cellar that had been built to preserve the hole in the earth where the two women and eleven children were killed by the Colorado militia and Rockefeller's goons.

The sun was purple in the west, the snow scarlet on the mountain peaks, the hardpan black with shadow, a cold, dusty smell like alkali in the air. The crowd lit their candles, and a Catholic priest with a microphone said a prayer in English and Spanish for the dead miners and their families. The waving yellow glow of the candles on the faces of the two hundred people was the greatest spiritual moment I'd ever known. Jo Anne squeezed my hand, and I knew she felt the same way.

The faces of the people could have come from a Bruegel painting—leathery and work-worn and inured by hardship. Their story was also written in their clothes. The colors were mismatched. Women wore men's coats. Almost all of them wore tennis shoes. Nearly every couple had children with them, in their arms or around their knees. Most of them did stoop labor and other kinds of backbreaking work but were fat because of their diet. If ever there was a group that resembled Jesus's early followers, I suspected I was looking at it.

Afterward, a union leader from California made a short speech and gave everyone directions to a dinner at a Catholic church a few miles away. The church was old and small and made of stucco and had settling cracks around the windows and all the other marks of an impoverished parish. Next door was a grammar school with a cafeteria, the serving tables loaded with food. As we were walking to the cafeteria, I saw a school bus turn off the highway and pull into the pasture that served as a parking lot. Marvin was behind the wheel and the first down the steps. He had shaved off his beard, giving his face a liberated look, in his case the angularity of an ax blade. A man I couldn't see clearly followed him down the steps, then the girls and Stoney.

"Who's the guy with Marvin?" Jo Anne said.

"I don't know. Don't pay attention to them."

"How does anybody survive tattoos like that?" she said. "His neck and throat look like a chunk of sewer pipe."

I couldn't resist and turned my head. The man's arms were too short for his torso, his throat tattooed with wraparound dragons, his dark hair greased and combed straight back, his biker vest and low-rider faded jeans and stomp-ass combat boots a message to the unwary. He swept up both Orchid with her purple-and-green hair and drooping eyelid, and Lindsey Lou with her pigtails and cowgirl clothes, as though they were collectibles he had won at a carnival.

He was a man I had never wanted to see again.

Jo Anne and I went into the cafeteria. The tables were crowded, with children running between them, the air filled with the smell of onions and chili and tamales and Spanish rice.

"That guy is staring at us," Jo Anne said.

"Don't look at him."

"You know him?"

"No. Let's get in line. You want a soda?"

"He's coming over," she said.

I pretended to wave at a union woman setting up a microphone on a stage, hiding my face behind my arm. Then I realized who I was waving to. "That's Dolores Huerta," I said.

"Who?" Jo Anne asked.

"Dolores Huerta. She cofounded the UFW with Cesar Chavez."

"Hey, Broussard!" the man from the school bus called out.

We were trapped in the line. He was now just a few feet from us. I tried to keep my eyes on Dolores Huerta. Then he was inches away. His odor was a combination of garlic and beer and hair tonic and machine oil and maybe an attempt at soap and water; he was a man who carried his environment with him.

"Broussard, right?"

"Excuse me?" I replied.

"You heard me. You're Broussard?"

"That's right."

"You don't remember me? I changed that much?"

"I'm not sure."

"Jimmy Doyle. Seventh Division, Alpha Company, second platoon." He leaned close to my ear and whispered, "Nine years ago, chasing nook and shooting gook."

"You've got me mixed up with somebody else."

"Summer 1953. You and that other kid from Texas were always together. See one, see the other."

"Wish I could help you."

"What is this, man? You blowing me off?"

"No, sir."

He looked at Jo Anne. "He's pulling my leg, right?"

"He's not a leg-puller," she said.

He took a comb from his back pocket and clawed it with two hands through the thickness of his hair, then examined the comb and returned it to his pocket, not once looking at me. "I think you're calling me a liar, Mac."

"Nope."

He huffed air out of his nose. "What was the name of that kid? He was KIA or got grabbed the night the gooks broke through on us. It was a funny name. Like a sword or blood or something."

"We've got to say good night, buddy," I said.

"I got it," he said. "It was Saber. Goofball Saber Bledsoe."

"We've got to move along, Doyle," I said. "That's your name? Doyle, right? Nice meeting you."

He surveyed the room, his face like a wax replica that had started to melt, his thoughts veiled. *"Okay,"* he said, as though he had just completed a conversation with himself.

"Okay, what?" I said.

"I give up." He looked at Jo Anne. "Enjoy your evening, pretty lady. Your guy is a lucky man. Watch out for him. He's a card." He walked away and squeezed Lindsey Lou and Orchid against his hips, swinging them in the air.

"You never saw him before?" Jo Anne said.

"I might have."

"Why didn't you just say that?"

"He's buds with Marvin. At best, he's hunting on the game reserve."

"What was that army stuff?" she asked.

"Who wants to find out? His tats are a nightmare."

She looked at me strangely. I thought I heard bugles in the hills, and wondered if they would ever cease. Through the back windows of the cafeteria, I could see electricity flaring on the horizon, like faraway artillery pieces silently lighting the bottom of the sky. I wanted the floor to split apart and swallow me alive and deliver me to a mythic garden between the Tigris and Euphrates when the world was only one day old and hung with fruit that had never been touched.

A boom of thunder rattled the windows, and a rush of wind slammed a side door into the wall and filled the room with the bright, cold smell of the storm. A solitary man was standing outside, his hooded slicker striped with rain. He pointed his finger at me and mouthed the word "you," as would a medieval inquisitor.

I went after him, into the ferocity of the night, the dust blowing, the snowcaps in the mountains turning to tinfoil, the parked gas-guzzlers and battered pickups shuddering with the velocity of the wind. The hooded man was gone. I wondered if I had become delusional.

I went back into the cafeteria, my clothes drenched, unable to explain my behavior to Jo Anne. "Don't worry about it, Aaron," she said, placing her hand on my arm. "Maybe he was someone who wandered in from the highway."

But there was no mistaking the apprehension in her eyes.

Chapter Seventeen

I DID NOT STAY over with Jo Anne. I not only felt embarrassed about chasing the man in the parking lot, I felt dishonest, even cowardly, about my encounter with the man named Jimmy Doyle. I was much like my father regarding those who seemed insatiable when it came to yesterday's box score. I never knew anyone who despised war more than he. His best friend, a boy with whom he grew up in New Iberia, Louisiana, was killed at my father's side in a trench on the morning of November 11, 1918, the day the doughboys thought the war was over. My father would leave the room, even a bar, the center of his addiction and the love and ruination of his life, when his friends' conversation turned to wars, past and present. He bore his friends no animus for their innocence, but he hated the Krupps and DuPonts of the world and the politicians who became teary-eyed and saccharine as they waved the flag and sent others to die in the wars they caused.

I despised the memories that lived inside me. I learned early in life that human beings are capable of inflicting pain on one another in ways that are unthinkable. I'm talking about a level of cruelty that has no peer among animals or the creatures of the sea. Once you witness it or, worse, participate in it, it takes on a life of its own, much like a virus finding a host. It burrows into your soul; it robs you of your sleep and clouds your days.

Weevils feed at your heart, and innocence and joy become the province of others. You live in quiet desperation and wake each morning with an anvil upon your chest.

If there are those who would argue with this depiction, I suggest they ask a man with the thousand-yard stare what kind of images he is viewing on the other side of his eyes.

I thought about all these things when I went to bed that night, as though picking reptiles one by one out of a basket and letting them strike my face before replacing them in the basket. I woke at four a.m. and saw Cotton smoking on his bunk in the dark, and wondered if he was chasing Waffen-SS through the catacombs, stenciling their blood with his grease gun above the tombs of Paul and Peter. I saw Spud walk to the latrine in his skivvies, his flip-flops slapping. I heard the snoring of America's undesirables up and down the row of bunks, then Spud's flip-flops as he headed back to his bunk and possibly his dreams about the prostitutes he had to pay to sing in his ear.

I slept for another two hours, then sat on the edge of my bunk, shivering in the coldness of the dawn, aching for Jo Anne's touch, wanting to smell her hair and kiss her hand and look into her eyes. I shaved and brushed my teeth and put on my clothes and went out the front door into the fog and the smell of woodsmoke and wet leaves and the coffee Chen Jen was boiling down at the dining hall.

Then I saw Jo Anne walking toward me in the fog. I was sure I was losing my mind.

SHE WAS WEARING a cute cap and a pink gingham dress and a charcoal-gray suede jacket and robin's-egg-blue tennis shoes without socks, as though she had pulled her clothes at random from a series of driers in a washateria. A thermos hung from one hand and a metal lunch box painted with the faces of Roy Rogers and Dale Evans hung from the other. "What's going on, big boy?"

"What are you doing here?" I answered.

"Thought you'd like to take a ride."

"Where?"

"My house. I have a present for you."

"What's going on, Jo Anne?"

She tossed me the thermos. It was heavy, and I barely caught it. "I'm going to straighten you out," she said. "What do you think about that, Buster Brown?"

A dense white fog was rolling on the stream that ran through the center of Mr. Lowry's property. I could smell the German browns and brook trout spawning inside the fog. They were the only trout that spawned in the fall, and the cold, fecund odor was of a singular kind, like a conduit into creation, the iridescent spray off the boulders so mysterious and lovely and improbable that I wondered if it was borrowed from a rainbow. Or maybe that was just the way I thought about things when I was with Jo Anne.

She opened the driver's door of her car and threw the lunch box on the seat. "Daydreaming?" she said.

"What's in the lunch box?"

"A scrambled-egg sandwich."

She started the engine but didn't put the transmission into gear. She ran her nails through the back of my hair. "You trust my driving?"

"Sure."

"How about in other things?"

"Yes, I trust you in all things."

"We'll see about that."

I had no idea what Jo Anne was up to. We drove down the

dirt road through the fog and rumbled across the cattle guard. In a half hour we were at her house. The sun was orange, the wind cold, the sky blue. I had already eaten the sandwich and drunk half the coffee in the thermos. "Thanks for the breakfast," I said.

"*De nada,*" she said, cutting the engine.

We went inside. Plyboard was still nailed across the back windows that were probably broken by Darrel. "What happened to the glazier?" I asked.

"He said he'll get here when he gets here."

Somehow the cavalier remark of the glazier made me angrier than the probability that Darrel Vickers had vandalized Jo Anne's house.

"You have a number for this fellow?" I said.

"Get in the house and shut up," she replied.

AFTER WE WERE inside, she locked the door and pulled down the shades. "Marvin and the school-bus gang have a way of showing up when they're out of money," she said.

"How about Henri?"

"He knows better than to come around." She went into the sunporch. A painted canvas rested on her easel. "I don't know how good this is or if you'll be offended. But this is what I see when I look at you."

I had never had anyone draw or paint me. Nor was I ever enthusiastic about having my photograph taken, not even for high school or college albums. Now I was looking at myself through someone else's eyes rather than a camera lens. My face looked bladed, as though there were a sharpness in my soul, yet my expression was uncertain, perhaps expectant or distracted by a presence the viewer could not see.

In the background, a guitar was propped against a modest table with a portable typewriter on it, similar to the Smith Corona I had carried in my duffel for two years. A candle inserted in the neck of a wine bottle was burning on the table, the dried wax on the bottle like pieces of string tied with a series of knots. The mystery of the painting was not me, at least not directly. It was the candle flame that cast shadows on the back wall. The shadows were like the bars of a prison, only slanted.

"Aren't you going to say anything?" she asked.

"It's a great compliment that you would paint me, Jo Anne."

"What do you see there?"

"I'm not good at self-inventory."

"You remember when I said you were a strange one?"

"I have to admit that stuck with me."

"I was wrong. You're not strange. You're exemplary. You're incapable of deliberately doing wrong. It's not even a virtue with you. I think you were born full of goodness and have always remained that way."

"Oh, Jo Anne, that means an awful lot to me, but—"

"If you say what I think you're going to say, I'm going to hit you."

"That's definitely not necessary."

She pushed me down in a chair. "Stay here. I'm going to bring us some more coffee."

"How about it on the martial arts stuff?" I said at her back.

She ignored me and came back a few minutes later with the coffee on the tray, then put it on the floor and sat down in a straight-backed cane chair and seemed to lose her concentration. "I don't know how to approach this, Aaron. The man you saw in the hooded slicker? He pointed and said 'you'?"

"That's what it looked like."

"Why would someone do that?"

"Maybe he was telling me I was guilty of something."

"A total stranger?"

"That's what I felt."

"You were in Korea, weren't you?"

"If I was, I wouldn't talk about it."

"What was your friend's name? The one who was with you?"

"Saber Bledsoe."

"He was killed?"

"He was listed as MIA. There were four hundred POWs not accounted for after the war. Maybe they were moved across the Yalu and used in medical experiments. Maybe Saber was one of them."

"Why are you hiding all this?"

"I don't like to talk about it," I said.

"You have to."

"Wrong."

"I'm not going to put up with this, Aaron," she said. "You're killing yourself, which means you're killing me."

I looked at the re-creation of my face on the canvas and the typewriter that never produced a publishable story and the burning candle that consumed itself in order to become a knotty pile of wax and the shadows that became prison bars.

"I didn't mean to say that, Aaron."

"Didn't mean to say what?"

"About you killing me. You're the only person in my life."

"That's not true. People love you."

"But you're the one. You know what that means, don't you? When a woman says it?"

"I'm just the way I am, Jo Anne. There are things I can't get out of my head. I think I'll always be like that."

"What things? The war?"

"It's what I did in the war. Or rather, what I didn't do."

"Then say it."

The metal band that had been my companion for many years was back in business. I don't think I have described it adequately. It had a turnscrew on it and was operated by someone I never had the opportunity to see. But he was a master. I felt him turning the screw, crushing my skull, shutting down the flow of blood to my brain. My eyes were jittering.

"Maybe I bugged out."

"You did what?"

"That means run for the rear. I was running, and an artillery round knocked the breath out of me. Saber was behind me. The Chinese were throwing grenades we called potato mashers. They'd clank them on their helmets to set the fuse, then throw them. But their flamethrowers were exploding the potato mashers before the fuses could. It was like being inside hell. I'd lost my steel pot and my rifle. I got up and started running again. I didn't go back. I left Saber behind."

I was weeping now, uncontrollably, my head down, my hands cupped like claws under my thighs.

"Aaron?"

I couldn't answer.

"Aaron, listen to me."

I saw her shadow on the floor, saw it come toward me and fall across my face and body. I felt her hand touch my head, then stroke my hair. "You're brave now, and you were brave then. You didn't desert your friend. You ran from the flames and explosions and probably certain death. You think your friend would have wanted you to do differently?"

I wiped my face on my sleeve. "I apologize."

"Don't say that. You're the most kind and good man I've ever known. You don't know how much you mean to me."

I looked up at her. Her image was out of shape, her hair hanging forward, her mismatched clothes the most beautiful I had ever seen on a woman. She wrapped her arms around my head and pressed it against her breast and kissed my hair. "I love you, Aaron Holland Broussard. You'd better believe what I say."

I don't know how long I held her. But I know it was a very long time.

Chapter Eighteen

WE HAD LUNCH together, and that afternoon she went to work at the hamburger joint and I went back to the bunk-house. I took my Smith Corona from under my bunk and set it on a small table by a window that gave good light throughout the day. I pulled a chair to the table and sat down and fed a piece of clean typewriter paper into the carriage and began typing. There is no more grand moment in a writer's life than typing the first sentence of a new book.

"Whatcha doing?" a voice said behind me.

"Hello, Spud," I replied, folding my hands in my lap. "What's happenin'?"

He was wearing pressed slacks and a strap undershirt, a shaving mug in his hand, his hair wet and his body still glowing from a hot shower. "I'm going to a movie in town with Maisie and a couple of others. Wanna come along?"

"I'm picking up Jo Anne after she gets off work," I said. "What happened to your face?"

"Miz Lowry put me to work trimming back her rosebushes."

I nodded at the page in my typewriter. "I'd better get on it."

"See you around," he said. He whistled a tune down the hall-way and into the latrine.

An hour later, I looked out the window and saw Wade Benbow's unmarked car coming down the road. I rolled my paper out of the typewriter and placed it in a manila folder and set on top of it a rodeo buckle I used as a paperweight. I walked out to greet him, my hands in my back pockets, the sun warm on my skin. I wanted to freeze-frame the day and not let it grow one second older.

He drove onto the grass and got out. "Know a kid goes by the name Moon Child?" he said. "One of those beatniks on the bus?"

I DIDN'T WANT TO hear his account, in the way you don't want to know what happened to an impaired person you watched walk through traffic when perhaps you could have pulled him back to the curb. I'm sure Wade Benbow took no pleasure in the words and images he used to describe the events that occurred in the early hours that same day, deep in the foothills of the Sangre de Cristo Mountains and west of Ludlow and the site of the 1914 massacre. And I'm sure, as a liberator of a Nazi extermination camp, he did not enjoy passing on more evidence of his fellow humans' taste for cruelty. But that's what he did, then coughed into his hand after he finished.

"Is she going to make it?" I asked.

"I don't know if she wants to."

"Somebody found her on the ground? By herself?"

"The guy who called it in wouldn't give his name. The dispatcher said he sounded like a broken record."

"But somebody saw the bus leaving the area?" I said.

"It fits the description of the one at the Farm Workers dinner. You saw it at the dinner, right?"

"Yeah," I said.

"So they must have gone from the dinner back to Ludlow," he said. "Why would they do that?"

"Have you talked to the others?"

"I've got them all in jail, but they're not saying anything. I have to turn them loose in twenty-four hours. There's a guy named Jimmy Doyle among them, a real hard case. Ever hear of him?"

"I talked with him at the dinner. He said he was in Korea."

"What's your take on him?"

"Bad news."

"This guy Marvin Fogel, the driver. He seems wired out of his head."

"They all are," I said.

I don't know why, but both of my hands itched, as though I had a rash or had been weeding a garden without gloves and had raked my skin with thorns. I could feel Benbow's eyes on me. "What are you not telling me?" he said.

I glanced up the grade at the Lowry house and the rosebushes in Mrs. Lowry's flower beds. "Nothing," I replied. "Let me get my coat."

MOON CHILD'S HEAD and most of her face were encased in bandages. Her arms were striped with bruises where she had been held by someone who had vise grips for hands. Her teeth and ribs were broken, her lips split. She was on a catheter, and a needle was taped to a vein in her forearm. Her face twitched each time she inhaled.

I sat in a chair two feet from her pillow. "I'm sorry this happened to you, Moon Child," I said.

Dried mucus clung to the corners and lashes of her eyes; I could hardly see them inside the depth of the bandages. "Did Marvin do this to you?" I said.

No answer.

"I met Jimmy Doyle, Moon Child. Maybe he's an okay fellow. Or maybe not. What do you think?"

I saw the fingers of her right hand move on the sheet. I picked them up as I would a handful of broken Popsicle sticks. "Want to tell me something?"

Her lips moved, but no sound came out. The sutures in them were black and as stiff as wire. I lowered my ear to her mouth. "Say that again?"

Her breath was like a tiny feather on my skin. I raised my head and eased my hand from under her fingers, then stood up. Benbow looked at me, his face a question mark. I pointed toward the door.

Outside the room, his right foot was tapping with expectation. "What'd she say?"

"She said, 'Where did Daddy go?'"

His face was drawn, his eyes empty. He reached unconsciously in his shirt pocket for a package of cigarettes that wasn't there. "I'd appreciate you coming down to the jail."

"What for?"

"I can't understand what the beatniks are saying."

THE HOLDING TANKS for women and men were at opposite ends of the same corridor. Our first stop was at the women's unit. Because it was a weekend, the room had a high occupancy. Most of them were DWIs and working girls and street drunks and women who were passed out for undetermined reasons and looked like they had been poured on the concrete floor. Orchid and Lindsey Lou were standing in a back corner, leaning into each other as though escaping a cold wind, their heads bowed.

I asked Benbow if we could talk to the girls in private.

"They won't come out," he said.

"Hey, Orchid!" I said.

No response.

"How about you, Lindsey Lou? Can you talk to me?"

They crouched together as though trying to burrow inside each other.

"Moon Child talked to me," I said. "Can't y'all do the same?"

They looked at me, then at each other.

"That's right," I said. "It took all her strength to do it. Give me two minutes."

They hooked hands and walked to the bars. The other prisoners pulled away from them. Orchid had tied her green-and-purple-streaked hair on top of her head. Her drooping left eye had a raw scratch under it. Lindsey Lou curled her fingers around the bars and pressed her narrow face, even her pigtails, between them, as though she wanted to squeeze herself onto the other side of the earth.

Orchid spoke first, her words hardly audible.

"You'll have to speak louder," I said.

"Is Moon Child dead?" she whispered.

"No," I said. "She's brave. So are you, Orchid. Who hurt your friend?"

"I didn't see anything," she replied.

"How about you, Lindsey Lou? Can you help Moon Child?"

"Is she gonna live?"

"I don't know," I said. "She wants her father. That means she wants to live. You have to help her do that."

"Nothing happened on the bus," Lindsey Lou said. "Marvin says there was a little accident. I was asleep. That's all I know." She twisted her face away, her chin in the air.

"What kind of accident?" I asked.

"I just told you I don't know," she said.

"Y'all know who did this," I said. "You have an obligation. Don't let your friend down."

Both of them stared at the floor. When they raised their faces again, their eyes looked like inkwells, and I was convinced no force on earth could pry the truth from them. But I tried. "Was it Marvin?"

"Marvin takes care of us," Orchid said. "Unless we're bad."

"What does Marvin do when you're bad?"

She folded her arms across her chest and lowered her eyes.

"Does Marvin punish you when you're bad, Lindsey Lou?"

"We love Marvin," she said.

"What about Jimmy Doyle?" I said. "Is he a grand fellow, too?"

"Don't say any more," Orchid said to Lindsey Lou. "He's trying to trick us."

"No matter how bad this seems, you can walk away from it," I said. "You've committed no crime. You can be a friend to Moon Child. Just tell the truth."

"Get away from us," Lindsey Lou said.

I saw Orchid's eyes take on the same hard look as her friend's. "Lindsey Lou is right. You're the enemy. You work for *them*."

"Who's 'them'?"

"*Them*," Lindsey Lou said. "Are you stupid? *Them*."

Wade benbow and I walked to the men's holding tank at the far end of the corridor.

"What's that about an accident?" I said.

"You got me," he said. "None of what they say is reliable, even when they think they're telling the truth. You know the real problem?" He waited until a trusty passed us with a food cart, then another with a mop and bucket on wheels. "The drug culture is just getting started. Middle-class kids are the target, and flatfeet like me are anachronisms."

A uniformed deputy caught up with us. He was holding two pages taken off a teletype machine. "Your request from the feds came in," he said. "Willie Sutton's legacy is safe."

Benbow skimmed over the pages. "I see Marvin Fogel here. There's nothing criminal on Doyle?"

"Read his two-fourteen," the deputy said. "A discharge for the convenience of the service. That's it."

The deputy walked away. A "convenience of the government" separation from the service could mean anything; 214 was the number of the form.

"What's Marvin Fogel been in for?" I said.

Benbow looked back at the pages. "Everything these clowns do. Mostly misdemeanors. Six months in Chino for shoplifting."

"I don't get it about Doyle," I said. "He has 'jail' written all over him."

Benbow looked at the pages again. "I hate to tell you the rest of it. The guy has a Bronze Star and was trained as an M.P."

Chapter Nineteen

MARVIN FOGEL WAS sleeping in an embryonic ball on a concrete bunk in the men's tank. Stoney was talking to a ballpoint drawing of Kilroy on the wall. Even though the room was cold, Jimmy Doyle was sitting shirtless and without shoes on the bare floor, playing cards with four other men. As soon as he saw me, he was on his feet, the veins in his chest and neck and upper arms cording like green spiderwebs.

"You cocksucker!" he said. He reached down on the floor without bending his knees and picked up a tin cup and flung it at the bars. "I should have known."

"Known what?" I asked.

"You dropped the dime on me."

"You got yourself here, Doyle."

"I remember you better than you think, Broussard. You screwed up at the listening post. You brought all that firepower down on our heads."

"Did you see Moon Child before they put her in the ambulance?" I said.

"That little bitch with the bangs? No, I don't know anything about her. I went to sleep. When I woke up, the bus was empty. Wait till I get you outside, motherfucker."

"Why do you have an interest in the Ludlow Massacre?" I said.

He got closer to the bars, his blue jeans buttoned just below his navel, his skin as smooth as an olive, his short arms pumped like bowling pins. "News for you. I couldn't care less about a bunch of Communists who got killed fifty years ago."

"You ever shoot crank?" I said. "I hear it turns your head into a pinball machine."

His eyes were fecal brown, lidless, the pupils dilated into black headlights. "You're gonna wish you were back at Pork Chop Hill."

I leaned against the bars, my head down. I stayed that way a long time, at least in terms of the situation. Why is that? The greatest fear and frustration you can engender in a man like Doyle is to ignore his rage.

"Sorry you feel that way, Doyle," I said. "I hope things work out for you."

Then I left him hanging on the bars and walked down the corridor and didn't stop until I was out of his view. Benbow caught up with me. "What's the deal?" he said.

"Can you get Stoney out of there without getting him in trouble?"

"The kid with porridge for a brain is going to help us?"

"Yeah, I think he will."

He rotated his short-brim Stetson on his finger. "Let's get a cup of coffee," he said. "I've been up since four."

WE GOT IT out of the machine by the dispatcher's office. It tasted like shellac. Benbow waited fifteen minutes, then sent a deputy down to the men's tank. I could hear the deputy's voice in the corridor: "Let's go, kid, you got your phone call."

"Don't got a phone call . . . Don't got a phone call . . . Don't got a phone call," Stoney replied.

"You get it whether you like it or not," the deputy said. "Stop talking to the wall and get your ass out here."

Benbow and I walked Stoney into an interview room and closed the door behind us. "How you doin', partner?" I said.

He was wearing a Mickey Mouse T-shirt and polka-dot tennis shoes and purple corduroy pants that were too big for him. I had never seen eyes so blue, so untroubled by knowledge or even awareness of the world. It was hard to separate Stoney's eyes from the fear and disorder that obviously held sway over his metabolism, if not his soul.

"They got you in here, too, ice cream guy?" he said.

"On an earlier beef, but I'm okay now," I replied. "Can you tell us what happened to Moon Child?"

He looked like someone had touched him with a cattle prod. He began making a droning sound through his nose, like a car engine going uphill.

"I think you called the ambulance, Stoney," I said. "That's a real good thing you did."

The droning shifted into overdrive.

I ran my fingers down the inside of his arm. "Who's been shooting you up, partner?"

The droning turned to a moan, then he began to wheeze.

"This is Detective Benbow," I said. "He wants to help you. You didn't do anything wrong. You're one of the good guys. You hearing me on this? Who hurt Moon Child?"

He stopped moaning and started crying.

"Stoney?" I said. "You still with us?"

He leaned sideways and tried to look past me through a small window in the door. His eyes were furtive, like a child's. "Moon Child's in the coven."

I saw Benbow look at me.

"The coven?" I said.

"All the girls are in it. The boys aren't allowed."

"This is a new one on us, Stoney," I said. "What exactly does the word 'coven' mean?"

"The thing the girls belong to."

"I see," I said. "If you get out of here, where will you go?"

"The place on the other side," he replied.

"Which place is that?" I asked.

"The place where everybody goes."

"Can you tell me where that is?" I asked.

"Where the spirits are dancing."

Before I could speak again, Benbow raised his hand. "Who are these spirits?" he asked.

Stoney smiled. "Everybody knows *that*. The Indians."

Benbow leaned back in his chair. "With feathers and such?"

"Yes, sir," Stoney replied. "They're the ones building fires up in the cliffs. I've seen them."

Benbow's right hand was opening and closing on his knee, his discomfort more than he could hide.

HE WAS SILENT most of the way to the Lowry farm.

"Why did Stoney's mention of the Indians bother you?" I asked.

"Who said it did?"

"You told me the Comanche did some bad things up the hill behind your house."

"Yeah, that's what I said. I was speaking in the past tense. The Comanche are dead, we're alive. End of story."

"I think you're not being truthful with me, Wade."

"Good way to get yourself a pop in the face."

"You asked me to help you," I said. "You shouldn't be talking to me like that, sir."

He didn't reply. That was all right with me. I was sick of the conversation. We had reached the turnoff to the farm. A mile-long freight train was wobbling down the tracks, headed toward Ratón Pass and the grinding slide into New Mexico. For just a moment I wished I had high-balled on through Colorado on the flat-wheeler that had brought me to the Lowry farm. Were it not for Jo Anne, I might have given my jalopy to Cotton or Spud and climbed aboard a hotshot and let the *click-a-dee-clack* of the wheels roll my troubles away.

"I've seen them," Wade said.

"Say again?"

"I didn't see them just dancing, either. It was in the middle of the night. I saw firelight up in the trees. I thought maybe dry lightning had sparked a fire, except there hadn't been any lightning. I took a fire extinguisher up there and saw more than I was planning on."

I waited for him to go on, but he didn't. "What did you see, Wade?"

A solitary drop of rain hit the windshield. He leaned over the wheel, lifting his eyes at the sky as though hoping for a cloud to burst and drench the hardpan and the hills. "I told myself I had a nightmare, one that went back to the death camp in Germany. I'm going to keep believing that."

"What about Stoney's story?"

"He's probably on angel dust or brown skag or both. That coven stuff is dog shit."

"What were the Comanche doing behind your house?"

His eyes were shiny. "There's times when you don't want to belong to the human race. There're times when you'd rather eat a bullet than see certain kinds of things. Or talk about them. Now shut up."

———————————

BENBOW DROVE ME to the bunkhouse. I know I have concentrated on the conflicts of Wade Benbow. This is because I had not dealt with my own. Earlier in the day, Spud Caudill had told me he'd gotten the fresh scratches on his face in Mrs. Lowry's garden. How did a man who had spent a lifetime doing dangerous work of every kind manage to remodel his face pruning a rosebush?

"You got something on your mind?" Benbow said.

My heart was racing. "No."

"Then why are you looking at me like that?"

"No reason."

"A word to the wise. You're young. All these problems will drop away one day. Don't let the shitheads of the world pull you under with them."

"Thomas Aquinas?"

"I owe you one, kid. Watch your butt," he said, and drove away.

I looked up the grade at the Lowry house, its immaculate, lacquered, battleship-gray Victorian presence couched among flowers and forest greenery like a testimony to a more innocent time. But it was not a more innocent time, and the sweatshops and textile mills and coal mines and the murder of striking workers were far more honest symbols of the Industrial Age.

I walked up the hill, wondering how I would explain my presence without lying if Mr. or Mrs. Lowry came outside. I paused when I reached the piked fence and the flagstones that led to the gallery. I could see no one inside. The side yard, the one that had the most sun, contained a gazebo threaded with clematis and trumpet vine. There was a ladder by the side wall and a half-broken trellis leaning in pieces against it. Rose petals were sprinkled all over the grass and the bed.

The French doors opened. Mrs. Lowry stepped outside, her smile as encompassing as ever, her dull-red hair wrapped partially around her thick neck. She was drying her hands and wearing a sundress with no covering on her sun-freckled shoulders, even though she was in shade and the wind out of the woods was cold and damp.

"Mr. Lowry is not home now," she said. "Can I help you, Aaron?"

"Spud told me he was doing some garden work for you. I just wanted to make sure everything got done all right."

"Depends on what you call all right," she said.

"Something happened?"

"He fell off the ladder and brought the trellis down with him," she said.

She was beaming and as always smelled like a freshly baked cake. I looked away from her. "That sounds like Spud."

"Want to come in?"

"I'd better get back to the bunkhouse."

"I just made a big strawberry milkshake."

"I'd better run."

Her eyes intensified. "I'd sure like to share it with you," she said.

I know my face reddened. I couldn't help it. I looked up at the sky and the yellow-and-purple marbling in the clouds. "I think we're about to get hit with a gully washer. Jo Anne wants me to drive her to work this evening."

"Well, she's a very nice young woman," she said. "And you're a very nice young man." She winked. I could almost hear her eyelid click.

I walked back down the slope, my face burning. I wanted to airbrush the last ten minutes out of my life.

LATE SUNDAY MORNING, Spud stopped me on the way to my car. "Hold up, Aaron."

I pretended not to hear him. He shouted again.

"What's up?" I said, gazing at the dirt road that led to the highway, hating the thought of the conversation that was about to ensue.

"I just went up to Miz Lowry's to clean the flower bed and repair her trellis," he said.

I nodded and looked at my watch. "Good," I said.

His eyes went everywhere except my face. He picked up a pebble and threw it at nothing. "Miz Lowry said you were up there asking if I'd done my work satisfactorily. You been checking on me, Aaron?"

"Your face was marked up, so I just wondered."

"Wondered what?"

"I wondered what happened. So I found out. You took a fall off the ladder."

"I think you were trying to find out if I did something else."

"I'm not reading you, Spud," I lied.

"The heck you're not. Rich women can get a hankering, too. I was working here a long time before you were. I know some stories."

"I don't want to hear this," I said.

"I thought you were my friend."

"I am."

"Not no more," he said, kicking at the ground. "Not no damn more."

He walked away, his shoulders simian and his back humped, his brow furrowed under his fedora, like a modern-day Quasimodo in search of cathedral bells.

Chapter Twenty

THAT AFTERNOON JO Anne and I took flowers to Moon Child at the hospital. Her condition was unchanged. There had been no visitors, no telephone inquiries. In fact, no one knew her real name. The clipboard attached to the bed frame identified the occupant as "M. Child." She was in the ICU, so she could not have flowers in the room. We left them at the nurse's desk. We were on our way out when the nurse on duty called us back to her desk. She was an older woman and had an erect posture and bluish-gray hair. No one else was around.

"I know you," she said to me. "The last name is Broussard."

"That's right."

"I was in the ER when you came in. You had been severely beaten."

I didn't remember her, but I said I did.

"I belong to a church that has rather strict boundaries about certain things," she said.

"I don't know if I'm following you, ma'am," I said.

"My religion teaches that the deliberate denial of information to a person who should have access to it is the same as a lie."

"I understand," I said. "But I don't know how that fits in with my presence here."

"Rueben Vickers attacked you," she said. "I've known him all my life."

"I see."

"He was here. He looked in that poor girl's room. I'm talking about the girl named Child. I asked him what he wanted. He left without speaking."

"Was his son with him?"

"No."

"Thank you," I said.

"Be careful, young man. And you, too, young lady. Rueben Vickers has depths no one should test."

Jo Anne and I walked back to my car. The sky was dark, the clouds swollen with rain or snow, the Indian summer dying like the leaves on the maple trees. I had a terrible sense of ephemerality, maybe because of the injustice done to Moon Child, or the nurse's warning about Mr. Vickers, or the fact that there was no way to hold on to the season and prevent the coming of winter.

Jo Anne's hair was blowing in a skein on her face, causing her to constantly brush it out of her eyes. "Why are you always staring at me like that?"

"I don't know."

"Yes, you do. Get that smile off your face."

"I stare at you because I don't want you to get away."

"I look like I'm fixing to leave town?"

"Not if I have anything to do with it."

"Really?"

"Can I ask you something that's a little private?"

"Depends on what you're going to ask me."

"Okay, I won't."

"Private in what way?" she said.

"Will you marry me?"

She closed her eyes, then opened them again. "You ask me that just after we visited somebody who had her head caved in?"

"That's the point. Clocks don't wait on people."

Her hand rested on the handle of the passenger door. She looked drunk. "I don't know what to say."

"Think it over. Take all the time you want. A day or two."

"You're the weirdest person on the planet."

"In what way?"

She pressed her palms to both sides of her head. I guess I had that effect on people sometimes.

WHEN I DROPPED her off for work, she still hadn't answered my question. The sun was going down, the hamburger joint glowing with red-and-yellow neon in the drizzle. She opened the door to get out, a newspaper over her head. I hate to admit this, but I wanted to cry. "We'll have to talk later," she said. "Okay?"

"Sure," I said.

"I just can't think all this through right now."

"Roger that," I said. "I didn't mean to upset you."

"You're going to pick me up?" she said.

"Why wouldn't I?"

She shut the door and ran through a puddle into the building, splashing her tacky orange-and-black uniform. I started the car and turned on the wipers. I could see her squaring her cap and wiping her face with a paper towel behind the counter. I wondered how many people were aware how hard she worked to earn the little she had. I drove away into the darkness, the wipers slapping back and forth, my high beams lighting up an empty firehouse, a low-rent saloon with blacked-out windows, a shelter for vagrants vandalized with graffiti, the sidewalk littered with trash,

I knew my thoughts were going to a bad place. There is a

strange phenomenon among human beings to which most of us are susceptible. It's an affliction that contaminates our vision of the world and invades the heart and the mind and the soul. Its origins are always the same: the sudden recognition that you are unloved or, worse, that you are unworthy of love. When that happens, you sail your ship alone, with no harbor lights in sight and no companion except the wind.

I never had a big thirst for booze, although I drank more than my share of it. Anger was another matter. I knew how to get drunk on it. My mother's family, the Hollands, were indiscriminate when it came to shooting people: Mexicans at San Jacinto, Yankee infantry at Little Round Top, Comancheros along the Chisholm Trail, take your pick during the Sutton-Taylor Feud, the Katzenjammer Kids on the Marne, Hitler's panzer corps in the breakout at the Bulge. The only problem was they did it to themselves as well, usually drunk, with a pistol, and through the head.

I kept seeing Moon Child in the hospital bed—abandoned by her friends, probably brain-damaged, wondering where her father was. I also could not get the nurse's warning about Mr. Vickers out of my mind. Why had he come to Moon Child's room? Why hadn't he gone inside? Did he intend to do harm to her? Or did he have suspicions about his son, who was a suspect in the asphyxiation of a playmate years ago?

Maybe Rueben Vickers had gotten a pass for too long, I thought. I drove farther down the street into a section of town where the power had failed and all the lights had gone out and the streets were draped with shadow. The sun looked like a guttering candle at the bottom of a V between two mountains, then it slipped off the side of the earth, and a wind laced with rain and wet snow blew through the streets with such force that the street sign on the corner trembled on the pole. I made a U-turn and headed for the two-lane highway and the ranch of Rueben Vickers.

THE HOUSE WAS on a plateau, made of purple brick, flat-roofed and sprawling and utilitarian, with white garage doors on each end facing the front yard. A huge American flag with a spotlight centered on it flew seventy-five feet high on a silver pole, even though protocol required that it be lowered at sunset and never flown in the rain.

The barns were enormous and hung with lights, the three-sided hay sheds stacked twenty bales high. All motorized equipment was either tarp-covered or parked in a giant, well-lit aluminum building. When lightning struck the mountain behind the ranch, I could see the eyes and horns of hundreds of Angus down in a draw, the entire herd bawling as the thunder rolled through the canyons.

One of the garage doors was open, the ceiling lights burning. Mr. Vickers's yellow race car was parked inside, fresh tire tracks leading from the pea-gravel driveway onto the concrete pad. The driver's side of the car was scraped, the metal gouged, as though the hubs on a bigger and a more powerful vehicle had spun into it. I parked and cut my headlights. There seemed to be no security system in place at the Vickers ranch, no dogs, no locked gates, no nocturnal paid help. As the nurse at the hospital had suggested, I had the feeling that few people wanted to test Rueben Vickers's charity.

I got out of my car and ran for the porch. On the way, I got a better look at the damage to the side of the race car. The pattern was characteristic of a traditional sideswipe. The incongruity was the lack of a different color of paint.

I knocked on the door, then knocked again. Mr. Vickers

jerked it open, a piece of fried chicken in his hand. I could see his son and a woman at a table in the dining room. "You again!" he said. "Like bubble gum on my shoe. What are you doing here?"

"Passing by," I said.

"This some kind of scam? You trying to put something on us?"

"Yeah, I've got a beef with your son. For breaking Jo Anne McDuffy's windows."

"He didn't break any windows. Now get away from my door."

"Why don't you tell him to take the mashed potatoes out of his mouth and come here and defend himself like a man?"

"You by yourself?" he said, peeking around both sides of my head.

"Yep."

"You think you're gonna get a few bucks, right?"

"I wouldn't spit on your money, Mr. Vickers."

"Where you get off talking to me like that?"

"May I come in?"

"Is that one of Darrel's little friends?" the woman at the table said.

"No," Vickers replied.

"Ask him in or close the door," she said.

Vickers's face was knotted with consternation. He looked torn between shoving me into the rain or inviting trouble with his wife. "Come inside. And watch your mouth. Got it?"

I entered the foyer. Glass gun cases and the mounted heads of deer and elk and mountain goats and at least one moose lined the walls. The photos on the wall included Richard Nixon, Billy Graham, and Strom Thurmond. A large-print black Bible containing both the Old and New Testament lay on a small table under a lamp by the hall closet, the words "Bless Our Home" stamped in gold on the cover.

"What might your name be?" the woman said to me. Her hair was parted in the middle and pulled straight back; her features could have been shaped with a putty knife. She wore a black blouse with a white lace collar and had an animated sternness about her that suggested a conjugal situation similar to waking up each morning on a medieval rack.

"I'm Aaron Holland Broussard, Mrs. Vickers. I'm pleased to meet you."

"He's here about business, Dorothea," Vickers said.

"What kind of business?" she asked.

"I heard Darrel was in an accident out by Ludlow," I said. "I hope he's okay."

Vickers had gone back to the table and was still standing. He dropped his piece of fried chicken on his plate and wiped his hand with a cloth napkin as if cleaning a dirty wrench. "You talking about the damage to my race car? I got slammed up in a practice run at Castle Rock. This has got nothing to do with our son."

"Just tell him to get out, Daddy," Darrel said. "Take the quirt to him if you have to."

Mrs. Vickers tapped her spoon on the tablecloth. "Both of you calm down. What's this about a quirt?"

"I believe Mr. Vickers's race car was involved in an accident with a school bus," I said. "The one the beatniks ride around in."

"What beatniks?" she said. "Darrel, have you been hanging around with beatniks?"

"No, he hasn't," Vickers said. "And you get out of here, Broussard." He nailed me in the sternum with his index finger.

"No, we will finish this here and now," Mrs. Vickers said. "Don't lie to me, Darrel. Were you in an accident?"

"I was up by Ludlow. The bus came out of nowhere and hit me."

"Why were you in Ludlow?" she said.

"Trying to help those girls."

"What girls?" she said.

"I think they're runaways. I think bad guys are making them sell themselves."

His mother's eyes were blazing. "Is this true, Rueben?"

"Yes," he said. "We didn't want you to worry."

She looked at me. "See? You have your answer, Mr. Broussard. Would you like a piece of chicken?"

"I don't think so." I looked at the heads of the animals on the walls. "Did you know both the Old Testament and Saint Paul teach the protection of animals? Try the Book of Hosea 2:18. Or Isaiah 11:6–9."

"You're a bunny-hugger, huh?" Vickers said.

"Why don't you guys fence in a big area in the desert and hunt each other?" I said. "Declare a three-day open season on people, put your jockstraps on outside your pants, and blow your neighbors to shit."

"You get out of this house," Vickers said. His son was rising from the table, a fork in his hand.

"You went up to Moon Child's room, Mr. Vickers," I said. "Did you want to see the job finished?"

He clenched my arm with one hand and tried to work me toward the door. Then I did something I had never done with an older man. I ripped his hand from me and slammed him against the wall. "If you ever touch me again, I'll tear off your arm and kick it up your ass," I said. Then I slammed him into the wall again, shaking the glass of his gun cases. Mrs. Vickers's mouth hung open.

I went out the door, the rain swirling in my face. I thought it was over. I should have known better. The greatest fear in men like Rueben Vickers is personal failure; they will destroy the earth rather than admit they're wrong. He came after me.

"Step back," I said, my car door half-opened.

"Apologize."

"Before you hit me with the quirt at Mr. Lowry's farm, you said your ancestors were burned to death by the Comanche. Is that true?"

His face was beaded with rainwater, his hair in his eyes. "What do you care?"

"I don't," I said. "I just thought you'd like to know they're still out there."

"You say the Comanche are still setting people on fire? Are you crazy?"

"I know two people who have seen them. They've heard their victims screaming."

"You're lying."

"They're coming for you, aren't they? That's what all this is about."

He put his hand in front of my face as though trying to push back my words. "You're a sick man," he said.

"What drives you, Mr. Vickers?"

"Get away from me."

"Your son put a playmate in an abandoned refrigerator, didn't he?" I said. "You can't get that image out of your head."

His eyes were ball bearings, his face peppered with rain. I got into my car and drove away. He never moved.

Chapter Twenty-One

THE RAIN WAS still falling when I picked up Jo Anne at eleven p.m. and drove her home. She hardly spoke. The headlights of other vehicles made shadows on her face like dark water running down window glass. I told her nothing of my visit to the Vickers home.

"Did you think over my proposal?" I asked, half-smiling, my throat catching.

"I've never told you a lot about my past."

"You mean with Henri?"

"With others as well."

"Yesterday's box score."

Wrong choice of words again.

"*What?*"

"That's a baseball term," I said.

We were stopped in front of her house now. I cut the engine and the lights. I hoped she was going to ask me in.

"I've helped you when you were in a bad place in your life, Aaron. Maybe you're mistaking that for something else."

"That's really dumb," I said. "The fact that you helped me is a positive, not a negative."

"I'm dumb?"

"I didn't mean it that way."

"I know," she said. Her hands were folded in her lap. "I'm really tired."

"Better get some sleep, then."

"We'll talk tomorrow, okay?" she said, opening the door.

"Sure. *Hasta la cucaracha* and all that kind of jazz."

"Why do you have to say that?" she said, and slammed the door behind her.

I drove to the bunkhouse and went to sleep in my skivvies with the covers over my head. I could hear the rain drilling the roof. Sometime in the early a.m. the rain stopped, and I woke up and went down to the latrine. Or at least I thought I did. Altogether too often in my life, I could not distinguish dreams from reality. When I was a young boy, I took my difficulty to my father; he told me that perhaps all of life was a dream inside the mind of God. That wasn't helpful.

On the return to my cubicle, I looked through the panes of glass in a side door in the hallway. Through the mist, I could see the Lowry house up the grade. A light was burning in one of the peaked towers. Steam was rising from the creek that ran through the property. I thought I saw the boss and horns of wild animals in the mists but could not be sure. I started back to my bed, then saw something from the corner of my eye that should not have been there.

Do you know the feeling I'm talking about? Caution tells you to flee and not let the flaws of the world possess you. But integrity and conscience tell you not to ignore danger any more than you would ignore someone breaking a bottle on a highway.

The moon had just broken through the clouds. A man in a hooded raincoat was staring straight at me. At first I thought he wore dark glasses. Then I realized his face was white, almost luminous, and I also realized he was not wearing glasses. His eyes were not eyes, either; they were sockets.

I rubbed my face and looked again. He beckoned at me as one would from the Great Shade. I twisted the doorknob slowly, automatically releasing the lock, and stepped outside. The air smelled like cistern water and mushrooms that bloom in forests that never see sunlight.

I have only minutes, he said.

Who are you?

I'm from the place where we all go.

You're the man they call Bible-thumping Bob.

Ridicule is the flag of cowards.

What do you want of me?

You're surrounded by evil forces. Your weakness is your guilt for events and deeds that are not yours to bear.

I think this is a dream.

But that does not mean it is less than true. Your father taught you that.

What? What did you say? Come back here and repeat that.

Then he was gone. I turned around and reached for the door. It was locked. Then I felt myself walk right through it and down the hall to my bed. At 0600, when I awoke, I was balled up under my blankets, my teeth chattering.

AFTER BREAKFAST, COTTON and a couple of Mexican wranglers and I went to work on Mr. Lowry's horses, twenty of them that needed their yearly shots and quarterly worming and grooming and hoof care and a penile procedure I won't describe. Spud walked down from Mr. Lowry's house chewing on a matchstick. "The old man wants to see you."

"What for?"

He tilted up the matchstick to a forty-five-degree angle with his teeth, then rolled it around with his tongue. "Got me."

"Is this about the rosebushes again?" I said.

"No, he asked me if you were out late last night. He must have seen you roaming around. How's it feel to have people check up on you?"

"What did you tell him, Spud?"

"I'm not my brother's keeper."

I took off my leather apron and walked up the grade to the Lowry house. Mr. Lowry was reading the newspaper on the veranda, wearing a straw planter's hat with a black ribbon around the crown. He lowered his paper. "Oh, hello, Aaron. Come into the library. Mrs. Lowry is shopping with Chen Jen this morning."

Why did I need to know his wife was away? "Is there something I can help you with, Mr. Lowry?"

"It's something no one can help me with. Nevertheless, I need to explain something to you. Now, come in."

His tone seemed totally foreign. I did not want to enter his house under the circumstances. I knew that whatever was on his mind would prove embarrassing for either him or me or both of us.

"Mr. Lowry, I was hoping to get all the horses back to the south pasture by noon."

"You're my foreman. Now please do as I ask."

I removed my hat as I followed him through the French doors into the library. I had seen the library through the door previously but had never been inside it. It was an extraordinary room, with floor-to-ceiling bookcases and deep maroon leather chairs and a large walnut desk and a framed antique map of Salem, Massachusetts, on the wall. There was also a telescope on a tripod by the French doors, one that could magnify either the heavens or the buildings at the bottom of the slope.

"I saw you standing outside the bunkhouse early this morning," he said. "Talking to a fellow I've never seen before. Want to tell me what that was about?"

"I thought maybe I had a dream about a man wearing a hooded raincoat," I said. "I had hoped that's what it was."

He sat down behind his desk and took off his glasses and cleaned them with a soft cloth. "I'm having a hard time sorting through that one."

"I have blackouts, Mr. Lowry. Not from alcohol. I go places inside my head and then wake up and can't remember where I've been. A lot of times I can't distinguish dreams from reality."

"Sit down. You want a sandwich?"

"No, sir."

"Whoever the man was, he was not here with my permission. Can you tell me the nature of his errand?"

"He said I was surrounded by evil."

"Let's see if I have this straight. This man with apparently no name or origins has come here to tell you that my farm, my produce, and my milk and feed business are evil?"

"He said nothing about you, sir."

He seemed to study the antique map on the wall. "This is more than I can deal with, so I'll say no more about it. If you see this man again, will you ask him to knock on my door? I'd love to meet him."

"Yes, sir."

He was smiling now, more like the man for whom I had such great respect. "Now let's talk about something else," he said. "Mrs. Lowry told me of your conversation with her."

I felt my heart slide into the basement. "I'm not much at remembering conversations, Mr. Lowry. Or talking about them."

"I have a medical condition that has taken its toll regarding my conjugal obligations. My wife has a great love of the world and the people who inhabit it. She made a mistake approaching you and admitted it to me. She respects you, as do I. We hope that respect is mutual."

"Yes, sir, it is. I don't even remember what was said. Jo Anne and I hold y'all in high regard." My batteries were down. I wanted to escape into the sunshine and the coldness of the wind and the blueness of the sky and the smell of snowmelt up in the trees, and most of all, I did not want to talk any longer with Mr. Lowry.

Then he said something I knew I would never forget, like dirt you can't wash out of your mind. "I want your promise," he said.

"Sir?"

"I want your promise you will never indulge in gossip about Mrs. Lowry."

My stomach had a hole in it.

"Did you hear me, Aaron?"

"No, sir, I didn't."

"You're suddenly hard of hearing?"

"My hearing is fine, Mr. Lowry. There are instances when I choose not to hear others. Thank you for inviting me to your home. I wish my father were here. He was something of a historian. He would have enjoyed talking with you about the Puritan artifact on your wall."

"Are you mocking me?"

"No, sir. I was just talking about my father and history and all that kind of thing. My best to Mrs. Lowry." I went out the door and down the slope, my head as weightless as a helium balloon.

Cotton and Spud and the Mexicans were waiting on me. They had fixed cowboy coffee in a big tin pot and stuck it in the warm ashes of a driftwood fire and were now sitting around the fire, drinking out of tin cups, all of them smoking roll-your-owns, probably donated by Cotton. But their mouths were turned down at the corners, their eyes avoiding mine.

"Somebody die?" I said.

Spud pulled a telegram out of his back pocket. He had been sitting on a log, and the telegram had been cupped stiffly into the shape of a half-moon. He handed it to me. "Chen Jen brought it up with the mail. I hope it isn't bad news, Aaron," he said. "You've always been my buddy."

"I appreciate that, Spud," I said.

"Last time I got one of those things, I ended up in khaki underwear," he said.

I worked my finger inside the envelope and tore it along the top, then read the strips of typed words that were glued onto the paper. I read them a second time and refolded the paper and placed it and the envelope in my pants pocket. I tied on my farrier's apron and pried up a mare's hind foot between my legs and began rasping her hoof.

"Everything okay?" Cotton said.

"I have a literary agent in New York. He said a publisher just bought my novel."

"Son. Of. A. Bitch," Spud said.

"You can say that twice," Cotton said.

The Mexicans were smiling, too. Spud began to dance around the fire, balancing his tin cup on top of his fedora, whooping like an Indian. "Ain't that something?" he said. "I always knew you had it. Ain't it funny how things work out?"

Chapter Twenty-Two

Aᴏᴛᴇʀ ᴡᴏʀᴋ, I showered and put on slacks and a dress shirt and a sport coat and drove to Jo Anne's house. It was a grand evening. Indian summer was back, and a song played in my heart. I was going to be a published novelist. When I arrived, the last rays of the sun had filled the clouds in the west with a golden light. I cut the engine on my car and got out with a solitary rose wrapped in green paper that I had bought from a street vendor. Then I saw the school bus parked in the field and heard someone hammering in back of the house. Jo Anne walked out from behind the house, carrying a bottle of Tuborg. She was wearing jeans and beat-up cowboy boots and was not dressed for the place I planned to take her.

"What are you doing with the Tuborg?" I said.

"Putting it in the trash for Henri."

"Devos is here?"

"He's fixing my windows."

"What else does he plan on fixing?"

"Quit it, Aaron."

"I'm sure this is a nightmare and I'll wake up any moment."

"What am I supposed to do? Throw him out?"

"No need. I'll do it for you."

"A couple of days ago he repaid two hundred dollars of what he owed me. He's trying to make up for his mistakes."

"Maybe the Vatican could give him early canonization. What's up with the bus?"

"Henri came here with them. They've joined up with some Buddhists. They might go up to Boulder."

"Is the Dalai Lama on board?" I said.

"I know you're mad at me for not giving you an answer about getting married. Don't take it out on others."

I had not told her about the sale of my novel. I wanted to place it like an emerald in her palm. I wanted to tell her I was going to dedicate it to her, then tell her about the new novel I was starting. Instead, I could feel a rumbling in the earth, a train going through my head, my paper-wrapped rose the scepter of the court fool.

"I'll get dressed," she said.

"Forget it," I said.

"You're acting like a child."

"Probably," I said, no longer looking at her.

Her eyes followed mine to the bus and the man who had just opened the front door and was swinging off the handrails onto the ground. "Don't go near that man, Aaron."

"Why not? He's buds with Henri, isn't he?"

"Please," she said.

"I bought this rose for you," I said. "Here."

Then I went to my car and reached under the driver's seat. She followed me, rising up on her toes, trying to see past my shadow. "Is that a gun?"

"Yes indeedy," I said.

"What are you doing, Aaron?"

"I don't know. I think I feel a spell coming on. Tell me how it works out, will you?"

I stuck the .38 Police Special in the back of my belt and walked to the bus. Jimmy Doyle, the man who could not let go of Pork Chop Hill, stood barefoot and bare-chested under the bus's row of windows, an unlit cigar inserted in the center of his mouth. His smooth olive-colored skin was painted with the sunset. He looked like a player on the Elizabethan stage, waiting for the audience to plumb his depths. The windows were crowded with the Greek chorus, mostly female. I didn't see Stoney or Orchid or Lindsey Lou among them.

"What's shakin', Doyle?" I said. "Loading up at the day-care center?"

"Beat it, fart."

"You said you were going to dust me when you got out of the bag."

"I didn't phrase it that way."

"Now is your chance."

"I'm simpatico here, Jack."

"I'm not. I don't like you."

"I'm all busted up on that."

"You hurt young people."

"Yeah? They don't look like they're hurting to me," he said. "Maybe that's because we're a family." He popped a match with his thumbnail and touched the flame to his cigar, his eyes hooded. "You got nothing to say?"

"No, I guess not. To tell you the truth, I'm out of gas."

"I saw you looking for something in your shit-mobile. You find it?"

I lifted the .38 from the back of my belt, my finger outside the trigger guard. I tilted up the barrel so he could see the shells in the chambers. "Want to hold it?"

He took a contemplative puff off his cigar. "What I want is you out of my fucking life."

"You said Saber and I screwed up at the listening post. You said we got people killed."

"So fog of war."

"You're saying I got my best friend killed?" I said. "Don't look away from me."

Smoke was leaking from around his cigar. He took it out of his mouth. He had lowered his eyes. I saw his weight shift from one foot to the other, his chest rising and falling. A fly crawled across his face.

"Apologize to those girls up there," I said.

"Apologize?"

"For pimping them out."

"Who's bopping the teenage poon in the stucco house?" he said. "Not me. Could it be you?

"I'm glad you said that." I grabbed his right wrist and pushed the gun into his hand. Then I pulled the cigar from his mouth and slapped his face and shoved him against the bus and pinned him by the throat and stubbed out the cigar three inches from his eye. "Use the gun or apologize."

"You're a section eight, man."

"You got that right." I slammed his head against the bus, again and again, my fingers sinking deeper into the green-and-red dragons tattooed around his throat. Then I pulled him away from the bus and slammed him again. This time his eyes crossed.

"Apologize!" I said.

"No!"

I twisted his right wrist and forced the gun barrel upward and into the soft spot under my chin. "Pull the trigger or apologize."

"No."

I tightened my grip on his windpipe. He began to gurgle as his face turned color. I pushed the gun's muzzle deeper into my own throat.

"Pull the trigger. You can do it."

The people on the bus had ducked below the windows except for one. I heard a window in back drop to the sill, then saw Stoney's head and the top half of his body lean out like a broken jack-in-the-box. His face was streaming with tears. "Ice cream guy! Don't hurt him any more! It wasn't him hurt Moon Child! Don't do this no more, ice cream guy."

"Who hurt Moon Child, Stoney?" I said.

He jerked his head inside the window, almost guillotining himself. I let Doyle slide to the ground. He had wet his pants and was making a sound like someone sucking air and water through a garden hose. I eased the revolver out of his hand. The girls were at the windows again, their faces filled with dismay and disillusion, like they had aged years within a few minutes. "You okay, Doyle?" I said.

"What's it look like?"

"Who tore up Moon Child?"

"She tripped and fell. I think she tied her shoestrings together." His cheeks were unshaved and as gritty as emery paper. He started laughing and couldn't stop.

I saw Jo Anne out of the corner of my eye. "Give me that goddamn gun," she said.

I removed the shells from the cylinder and sprinkled them on Doyle's stomach. "Here," I said. "End of problem."

"You call this the end of the problem?" she said.

The sun was blood red between two mountains that seemed to teeter on the edge of the earth, as though the earth were not round but flat and precipitous and all of creation were about to slide into infinity. "Why did you bring Henri Devos back into our lives, Jo Anne?" I said.

"You've still got your mind on Henri?" she asked. "You tried to make a guy blow your face off, for God's sake."

The bus had started. Two boys naked to the waist, with skeletal rib bones and hair a foot long, picked up Doyle and dragged him through the side door. I watched the bus lumber across the field, the dust rising like wisps of smoke from the tires. Stoney's face was pressed against the back window, out of shape, like a plumber's helper, his arms pinned behind him by people I couldn't see, his mouth forming words I couldn't read.

I DROVE HOME BY myself, without saying good night to Jo Anne. My trip back to the Lowry farm was probably the loneliest of my life. The sky was black, the constellations cold and white from one horizon to the other, but I found no joy in them and certainly no light. Up on the hill, the Lowry house was lit as brightly as an amusement park, although I could see no cars parked close by.

"Mama Bear wants to see you topside," Spud said. He was sitting on his bunk in his skivvies, buffing his dress shoes.

"Mrs. Lowry?"

"In the flesh. Powder and perfume. I thought I was gonna pass out."

"She wants to see me tonight?"

"Want me to write it on the wall?"

"I don't need this," I said.

"Think about it. She's probably got the Grand Canyon under her dress." He looked up. "Sorry. I got a dirty mind."

I trudged up the slope and knocked on the door. She pulled it open slowly. "Ah, my darling boy is back. And so dressed up."

"I was going to take Jo Anne to dinner. It didn't work out. You and Mr. Lowry wanted to see me?"

"No, it was me who wanted to see you. Come in," she said.

She was wearing a dark purple Oriental silk dress with green flowers on it. Her skin was flushed, her dull-red hair tied up with a bandana, like a factory girl's. "You think I'm going to bite you?"

"I'm not sure."

"Sit on the couch. Don't talk until I tell you to. When I'm finished, you can be on your way. Or hang around." Her eyes crinkled.

"Is Mr. Lowry here?"

"Of course not." She pushed me on the couch.

"Mr. Lowry has already talked to me, Mrs. Lowry."

"And he probably left you more confused than ever. You're an intelligent young man. So I'm going to tell you things I don't tell other people."

I knew there was no way out of her house unless I listened. She sat down next to me with one leg folded under the other. She stroked my cheek.

"Mrs. Lowry, this is embarrassing," I said.

She leaned over and clamped my face in her hands and kissed me on both eyes. She smelled like a garden full of flowers. Then she let go of me with a loud "*Umph!*"

By that time I had realized that a grunt from Mrs. Lowry could mean almost anything but probably wasn't good. "Are you all right, ma'am?" I asked.

"I'd love to eat you up," she said. "You remind me so much of the son we lost at Guadalcanal."

I hated to think about the implications of that statement. "Mrs. Lowry—"

"Oh, be quiet. I have to speak with you about the unpleasant realities of commerce, so please put up with my little indiscretions. Since my husband is a gentle soul, I'm the one who has to take care of certain things. Our paradise in the Southern

Rockies is in jeopardy. The agricultural corporations are taking the meat off our bones." She picked up a strand of my hair and tugged on it. "Are you listening?"

"Y'all are going under?"

"Not if I can help it. Some call it making a deal with the devil."

"Ma'am?"

She drummed her fingers on the back of my neck. Her eyes were reddish brown, her smile both maternal and flirtatious, of the nature that can make a young man's viscera melt.

"What are you thinking?" she asked.

"Nothing. I'm a blank."

"Tempted a little bit?"

"I sure am. I'm not a well person, and I wish you'd stop this, Mrs. Lowry."

"I wouldn't hurt you for the world," she said. "But learn it now, Aaron, if you have money, people will do everything they can to take it from you. The Irish sailed here on the coffin boats and were treated like bilge when they arrived. Then they died in front of Confederate cannons, and not for the slaves, either, but to protect the profits of the textile mills. My husband's Puritan ancestors got off the *Mayflower* and set about murdering and spreading disease among the Indians, and when they ran out of Indians, they hanged their neighbors. That's the bloody truth. Don't be deceived by the nonsense you were taught in public schools."

"I can't keep up with you, Mrs. Lowry."

"A great change is occurring as we speak. Its origins are the Golden Triangle and Latin American."

"You're talking about drugs?"

"Marijuana, heroin, and cocaine. Great amounts."

"I'm not sure what you're saying."

"We own properties in northern Mexico and the Rio Grande

Valley. That's the equivalent of owning a subway between Mexico City and San Antonio. The traffic is mostly marijuana."

I couldn't speak. I thought I was having a dream. She ran her nails through the back of my hair. "Look at me," she said.

"Mrs. Lowry, please—"

"I just need a yes or no. Would you be willing to stay on with us, knowing what I just told you?"

"You're trafficking in drugs and telling me about it?"

"What's worse, drugs that do less harm than alcohol or the weapons we export all over the world?"

"I don't want anything to do with this, Mrs. Lowry."

She took her hand away. "You're a lovely boy. If my son had lived, I'd want him to be just like you."

I was sweating, my head pounding. I got up from the couch. "I wish you had never told me any of this, Mrs. Lowry."

"I haven't made a serious mistake, have I?" she said.

"Y'all have always treated me right. I'll always be in your debt."

"Translate that for me?"

"I'm saying good night. You have to pardon my physical situation. I think I had an erection. I'd like to kill myself."

"You're sweet, you surely are. Jo Anne is a lucky girl. Be gone with you, now."

I could hardly walk when I left the house. I wanted to rise into the stars and sail over the mountains. I wanted to escape into the world of my father on the banks of Bayou Teche and the night smell of magnolia or jasmine or trumpet vine or orange blossoms. I wanted to be anywhere except where I was. I felt I had just watched the destruction of paradise.

I cut through the yard, knocking into a birdbath and a sundial and tripping on croquet wickets that were pinned in the grass. A southbound train was blowing down the line. I saw myself on the floor of a boxcar, the wheels rocking on the tracks, Ratón Pass sliding past the open door, a rolled blanket under my head. All I needed to do was close my eyes and I would wake in Albuquerque.

Then I heard Mrs. Lowry call out from the doorway. The resonance and volume of her voice were operatic. "You're a babe among the heathens, Aaron."

Chapter Twenty-Three

THE NEXT DAY was Tuesday. I heard nothing from Jo Anne. Each time I started to call from Chen Jen's phone in the dining room, I could not erase the image of Jo Anne walking from behind her house the previous evening, a bottle of Henri Devos's Tuborg in her hand, as though the flower I had brought her and the dinner we had planned and my desire to marry her were inconsequential. Even worse, she seemed to have dismissed Devos's treacherous financial behavior and his exploitation of her innocence, as though she did not deserve better.

I was also having problems with Mrs. Lowry's revelation about her and her husband's willingness to involve themselves with Mexican drug traffickers. The respect I'd had for them was gone. I couldn't believe their naïveté, either. Have you ever taken a nocturnal excursion through the back streets of Tijuana or Juárez? What you see is not human. Forget nuance, latitude, social science, church-basement bromides. The worst that people are capable of is available for a few greasy coins. The violence imposed by the narco gangs on their enemies and sometimes on innocent peasants is something you never want to see or even know about, lest your faith in your fellow man fly away forever.

Even though we dug postholes all morning, I had no appetite when we went to the dining hall for lunch. I asked Chen Jen to make me a ham sandwich and sat down with Cotton and Spud.

"You don't look too good," Cotton said.

"I'm extremely copacetic."

"Your gal run off?"

"Mind your own business, Cotton," I said.

A new Classics Illustrated comic, *King Arthur and the Nights of the Round Table,* lay by his plate. He teased the cover and pages with his thumb, then rolled it up and took his plate to another table.

"Why'd you have to do that?" Spud said.

"I had a bad night. I got to ask you something."

"How to win friends and influence people?"

"You hear anything about drugs around here?"

"Those beatniks are supposed to use them."

"I'm talking about on the property."

"With Mr. Lowry running things? Who you kidding?"

I bit into my sandwich but couldn't swallow. I picked up the pitcher of Kool-Aid we always shared at the table and poured my glass full.

"What's eating you, Aaron?" Spud said.

"Everything."

"You shouldn't ought to have talked to Cotton like that. You and him and me are the Three Musketeers."

"You're right." I went over to Cotton's table and told him I was sorry.

"I didn't pay it no mind," he said.

"What you said was the truth."

"You got woman trouble?" he said.

"A mess of it."

"You love her?"

"Yes, sir, I sure do."

He stared at me with his good eye and his white eye at the same time, which was like looking at two different heads that had been sawed down the middle and glued together. "Then get your butt over to her house and tell her that."

"You belong back there with King Arthur's knights, Cotton."

"I hear that a lot," he replied.

I went back to my table and finished my sandwich and Kool-Aid, then went outside into the wind and the sunshine and started the day all over. Minutes later, I looked up from twisting the handles of a posthole digger in ground that was as hard as concrete, and I saw Wade Benbow's unmarked car coming up the road in a cloud of dust.

HE PUSHED OPEN the passenger door for me to get in.

"I'm working," I said.

"No, you're not. Get your butt in here."

"You're the second man in fifteen minutes to say something like that to me."

"It's about your girlfriend."

My viscera turned to jelly. I sat down on the passenger seat. The car stank of nicotine. An unfiltered cigarette was burning in the ashtray. "What happened?"

"She's okay. I mean physically. Y'all had a fight or something?"

"Yeah, *something*. Where is she?"

"At home." He reached for a notepad on the dashboard. "This is what I have so far. You were supposed to go out to dinner with her. The art professor was fixing her windows. The school-bus zoo was parked in the field. You got into it with this guy Jimmy Doyle. Then you left by yourself."

"That's right. Can you get rid of that cigarette?"

He removed it from the ashtray and threw it out his window. "Who would have reason to do Jo Anne McDuffy harm?"

"You said she was all right. How about telling me what's going on?"

"I didn't say her house was all right. Back to my question—who would want to hurt her?"

"I'd start with Darrel Vickers."

He scratched his forehead. "Yeah, that kid should have been lobotomized years ago. After you left, your girl decided to get in some extra hours at her job. When she came home, the windows in back were broken again, the interior was ransacked and smeared with feces, and all her paintings were stolen."

"The paintings she did about the Ludlow Massacre?"

"Yeah, it seems like a pretty hard blow for her."

I doubted if he had any idea how hard. It's the worst fear of every painter, every photographer, every sculptor, and every writer. I couldn't imagine what I would feel or do if someone stole or destroyed the only manuscript of my novel. "No witnesses, no clues?" I said.

"Nope. One other thing, though: I talked to the art professor. He said he left an envelope with four hundred dollars in it on the counter. Some kind of payback for a loan. I found the envelope on the floor." Benbow looked at his notepad again. "This is what he wrote: 'Here's the rest of the money I owe you and a little for interest. I will always remain your student rather than the other way around. Love, Henri.' The envelope was torn open and the cash taken. Got any thoughts?"

"Yeah, Henri Devos is the stink on shit. Where is Jo Anne now?"

"I'd try her house. It's going to need quite a cleaning."

"Where's this going, Wade?"

"You know the answer to that."

"Why are you still smoking?"

"It keeps my mind off chemo."

His package of Lucky Strikes was on the dashboard. I picked it up and got out of the car and flung it into the rain ditch. It sank among the cattails.

"You need to butt out of my life, Aaron."

"Is there any brown tar around here?" I said.

"Mexican skag?"

"That's what some call it."

"A musician here or there. Why?"

"No reason. How about angel dust?"

"Yeah, some," he said. "Let's go back to your question about heroin. You know something I don't?"

"I'm in a bad place," I said.

He gazed at the steely blueness of the mountains, the bales of hay lying in the fields, the Holsteins and red Angus and the white fences and the coffee-brown richness of the land that had been harrowed and the barns that were bigger than most houses and the pebbled, tree-lined stream that could break your heart. "Yeah, being young with your whole life ahead of you is a real torment, isn't it?"

Chapter Twenty-Four

I TOLD MR. LOWRY I had an emergency and needed to leave work early. "Anything I can help with?" he said in the kind way I always associated with him.

For a moment I wondered if he was unaware of Mrs. Lowry's pernicious activities on the border. Even so, I knew I would never be able to forget his request that I not tell others of her promiscuity. My relationship with him and my faith in people would never be the same. I thanked him for his offer of help, but I couldn't look at his eyes. I'd had the same level of respect for Mr. Lowry that I'd held for my father, and his inability to understand that increased the embarrassment and shame I felt for him.

I drove to Jo Anne's house. All the windows and the front and back doors were open. She was scrubbing the kitchen floor on her hands and knees, her hair tied up with a bandana. There were trash bags, bottles of Clorox, buckets of soapy water, mops, and brooms all over the house, and in the trash bags fecal-streaked clothes and broken plates and shattered glass.

She did not see or hear me walk in. I squatted down and placed my hands on her shoulders, then took the scrub brush from her and lifted her to her feet and put my arms around her. I could feel her blood humming. "Wade Benbow told me what happened," I said. "Why didn't you call me?"

"You left last night without even saying goodbye. All you seemed to care about was acting crazy."

"I felt hurt, Jo. I asked you to marry me, and you let a fraud and a cretin like Devos on your property."

"I guess I'm just not good at throwing people out of my house."

I pressed my cheek against the top of her head. "That's why I love you."

She didn't answer. I heard her sniff, then felt the wetness from her eyes through my shirt. "All my paintings are gone," she said.

"Benbow told me. We'll get them back."

"How?"

"The guy who did this plans to sell them. Otherwise, he would have destroyed them like he did everything else."

She rubbed the skin under her eyes with the heels of her hands. "Where would he sell them?"

"I don't know. But we'll find out. I promise."

Of course, I had no way of knowing if she would ever see her paintings again. But is there a greater sin than robbing people of hope, particularly when thieves who break in and steal have taken everything from them?

"Why would anyone smear my home with excrement? It's not dog feces, either. I think it's from a human being."

"We're talking about a sick person, Jo. That's how you have to think about this. The person who did this is not human, he's a disease. You don't hate a disease."

"You think it was Darrel Vickers?"

"He's a good candidate."

"Why just a candidate? Who else would do this?"

"Benbow said the intruder took the envelope of money Henri Devos left for you."

"That's right."

"And there was a note to you on the outside about the money?"

"Yes."

"That bothers me a little bit."

"I don't understand," she said.

"Why wouldn't the intruder just put the envelope in his pocket instead of tearing it open and throwing it on the floor, maybe leaving his fingerprints?"

"Maybe he had gloves on."

"If he had gloves on, he wouldn't waste time digging the bills out of the envelope. He would put the envelope in his pocket."

She looked into space, her eyes clouding, as though a fly had swum into her vision.

"What is it?" I asked.

"I didn't see the envelope until the cops got here. It was on the floor. Henri must have left it on the counter to surprise me."

"So you never saw the money?"

"No."

I looked away. The implications about the torn, empty envelope that had supposedly held money were coming together in her eyes.

"You're saying Henri did this?"

"I didn't say that, Jo."

"I can't think straight. Only a monster could do this. Henri isn't a monster."

"I know what you mean," I said disingenuously. "Look, let's get something to eat. Then I'll help you clean up."

"I wouldn't push this off on anyone," she replied.

"I'm not anyone," I said.

She sat down on a counter stool, her face listless, her mouth gray, the knees of her jeans soaked with water and Ajax and mop string that looked like dead worms. She blew out her breath. "Some fun, huh, boss?" Then her eyes closed slowly and her arm slipped off the edge of the counter. Her head jerked up. "Oh, sorry. I think I'm going to fall down. Before I do that, I need to ask something of you."

"What is it?"

"Stay with me. Don't go anywhere. Just stand there for a long time."

"Sure."

"Because I think I want to sleep and then do something awful. Did you ever feel that way? You know, to sleep and maybe die inside and then get up and hunt down someone and punish them for everything that's wrong in the world? I felt that way when my father was sucked away by the storm. I feel that way now. I feel like I'm at the bottom of a well. I'd like to borrow your gun and shoot someone."

I didn't know what to say. Nor did I want to hear the way she was talking. "We don't let the bad guys get to us."

"You said 'guys' instead of 'fellow.'"

"My agent sold my novel," I said.

Her mouth opened. "When?"

"I got the telegram yesterday. I'll receive a thousand-dollar advance, less the agent's ten percent. We're going to get your house repaired."

"Why didn't you tell me?"

"I saw you with Devos. I forgot."

She pulled open my shirt and pressed her face into my chest again, then began kicking my leg with her tennis shoe.

"What are you doing?" I asked. She said something against my chest I couldn't understand. "Say that again?"

Either she didn't hear me or simply refused to repeat herself. She wiped her face on my chest and stood on my shoes and put her arms deep inside my shirt and wouldn't let go.

LATER, WHEN SHE went to the store to buy more cleanser, I used her phone to call Wade Benbow. I told him about my suspicion regarding Henri Devos.

"You really think the guy's that bad? He'd rub his shit all over her house?"

"He might if that would put blame on someone else."

"I guess it's possible."

"It's *possible*? That's it?" I said.

"You know how many open homicides I have on my desk? Plus other matters, like why you were pumping me about the availability of brown tar around Trinidad."

"Somebody told me to expect it."

"Who's this somebody?" he asked.

"What's your attitude toward snitches?" I asked.

"I don't have one."

"You think of them as lowlifes. That's why you call them 'confidential informants.' Are you smoking a cigarette now?"

"You're about to tell me the tobacco industry does more harm than dope mules, right? You know what you can do with that?"

He was right about me. I didn't want to be an informer. Who does? Jo Anne's car was coming up the road. The sun was in the west, the sky purple, snow and rain blowing in her headlights.

"Don't mess with me on this," he said.

"Maybe it was just talk."

"I know you better than you know yourself, partner. You have a conscience. This is going to eat your lunch."

"I don't have any more to say on the matter," I said.

"You sitting down?"

"Why?"

He coughed slightly. "That kid named Moon Child?"

"What about her?" I said, my heart seizing.

"The nurse found her dead an hour ago. A pillow was on the floor."

JO ANNE CAME through the door clutching a bag of groceries and a jug of Clorox. She was smiling. I took the bag and jug out of her hands and told her what had happened. Or at least most of it.

"She's dead?" she said. "Moon Child died in the hospital?"

I told her about the pillow. She sat down at the counter. Her face was as colorless as cardboard, her hair hanging in her eyes. "She was murdered in the hospital? How can that happen? Where were the cops?"

"It's not their fault, Jo Anne."

"Nobody cared enough to find out her real name."

"She never told you what it was?"

"No, she said Marvin picked her up when she jumped out of a semi on the Pass. The driver tried to make her sodomize him."

"Marvin Fogel picked her up in Ratón Pass?"

"Wandering in the middle of the highway. She said he fed her and gave her clean clothes and money. She said Marvin was the only man who was ever kind to her."

"Did she ever say where she was from?"

"California, I think. She said something about Buck Owens and Bakersfield. She said she was going to be in the movies."

"In California?"

"No, Trinidad. A science fiction picture or something. She was going to play a goddess."

"She told you this when she was loaded?"

"All of them are loaded. If I grew up like them, I'd stay loaded, too."

"I need to find Stoney."

"The bus goes wherever there's free food." She stared at the floor, her defense system obviously used up.

The rain had stopped, but I could hear it dripping from the eaves and smell the coldness of the fog and the clean dampness of the earth coming through the broken windows. The sun was a whitish yellow, with the pale, thin fragility of a Communion wafer buried inside a cloud. I felt strange about Moon Child. She was the angriest of the kids I'd met on the bus, yet perhaps the one who had the most courage. How could she have been led on by a Hollywood con man claiming he could cast her in a movie?

I put my hand on Jo Anne's shoulder. "I'm going to call a carpenter friend of mine and hang some blankets over the windows, then take you out to eat. Is that okay?"

"Sure."

"Then we'll take a ride down to the Sally. They're good people."

"The what?" she said.

BACK THEN, WHEN you were on the drift, you learned quickly that the Other America was a complex culture held together by the poetry of Walt Whitman, the songs of Woody Guthrie, and the prose of Jack Kerouac. I knew former Wobblies and CCC boys who were still riding the rods, bumming their way from Ammon Hennacy's Joe Hill House in Salt Lake City down to the date-palm harvest on the California-Mexico border, their faces as lined as an old leather glove, most of them toothless, vibrating on the floor of a flat-wheeler, filled with joy from their first drink in the morning until they slept under the stars that night.

Marines never denigrate the Corps, not even brig rats who are kicked out of the Crotch. When it came to the Salvation Army, the fellows with their legs hanging out the side door of a boxcar had the same degree of loyalty. Hallelujah missions were everywhere on skid row, but the Sally was special. Their brass bands might deafen street drunks into ear-bleeding sobriety, but they were steadfast when it came to teaching the equality of women and people of all races.

The Sally in Trinidad was in the warehouse district. An ex-pug and two-time loser friend of mine who worked there told me he knew the crew on the bus well, but he had not seen them in three weeks. My friend, Jersey Joe Finkelstein, had the skin and light hair and eyebrows of an albino, and brain damage from either the ring or a blow from a piece of pipe in the state pen, whichever account you wanted to believe. He ate cough drops all day and breathed through his mouth when you talked to him.

"You know a kid on the bus nicknamed Stoney?" I said.

"Looks like he got shot out of a cannon yesterday, talks in overdrive or like he's got a Coke bottle up his ass?"

He was sweeping the sidewalk in front of the building while he talked. He looked around to see if anyone had heard his language.

"That's the kid," I said.

"Funny you mention him. He was the one on the bus I worried about. The girls would get by for reasons we don't need to talk about. But a boy like that usually ends up lamb chops, get me?"

"No."

He looked around again. "The shitheads running that bus are gonna keep the girls around for obvious reasons. Stoney is bait to get the girls on board. Is that your lady in the car?"

"Did you know a girl named Moon Child?"

"Bangs, a face like a white balloon, an attitude?"

"She was murdered."

"Oh, man," he said, squeezing his eyes shut.

"Know why anyone would want to kill her?"

He pulled up his T-shirt, even though the wind was raw, and wiped his face. "I don't associate with people like that. I work here now. I quit that running around."

"Come on, Jersey. I need a favor. You're a stand-up guy."

"There're two guys on that bus that need straightening out. Guys with three inches of dick and two of brain. You get the picture?"

"What are their names?"

"Marvin and Jimmy. They had a lot of camping stuff on the roof. They had something else up there, too: a big wood star. I asked them why they wanted a big star on the roof like that. Marvin said it was a *hexe*. I said, 'What's a *hexe*?' He just grinned at me."

"Think they're making a movie?" I asked.

"Yeah, me and Elizabeth Taylor are starring in it. Are you out of your mind?"

"Don't let Stoney down. He's a good kid. You said it yourself. Those guys will cannibalize him."

"I heard them talking about Ludlow and going on through the massacre site into some place around Cordova Pass and then way-to-shit on over in the Sangre de Cristos. You been in those canyons? You got to bring in the sunlight on a truck."

Chapter Twenty-Five

Each day after work, I helped repair the damage done to Jo Anne's house. A couple of afternoons, Spud and Cotton came along with me. Wade Benbow dropped by. Moon Child had died of suffocation. What else was new? Cynical? You bet. Most crimes go unpunished. All cops know that, and so do the victims. You just live with it.

The days were becoming shorter, the light colder and more brittle, and my idyllic life with the Lowry family was coming to an end. Even though I would receive part of the advance for my book, I did not have a great deal of money. However, that was far less of a problem than the loss in Jo Anne's eyes when she looked at the sunporch where she had kept her paintings.

It was Friday evening, and Jo Anne had the night off, and I was cooking tamales and eggs on her stove, a storm buffeting the window panes; Spud and Cotton said they might come over with a few beers and bring Maisie. I thought we might have a fine evening. Then, out of nowhere, Jo Anne said, "I painted the children inside the flames at Ludlow in order to release them from their pain. Now they'll never be free. Whoever stole my paintings will keep them inside the fire. Do I sound crazy?"

"No," I said. "You can paint the children again. The Man Upstairs gave you a talent for a reason. He's not going to take it from you."

"He took my father," she replied, her face pinched with anger.

Then I knew the source of our problem, the barrier that would always be there. I could be her companion, a confidant, an occasional lover, a witness to her aging process and finally her death, but I would never be *the one,* because he had already disappeared up a funnel into infinity.

"Why the look?" she said. "You don't think God did that to my father?"

"I've never understood the great mysteries, Jo."

She sat on a stool, her shoulders slumped. "I can't get the children out of my mind. I see the screams on their faces. I thought if I told the world what happened to them, it would make a difference." A wet line slid down from each of her eyes. "I don't know how human beings can be so cruel."

"Molly Brown was on one of the *Titanic* lifeboats," I said. "The water was full of drowning and freezing people. Everyone else on the boat, including a ship's officer, was afraid to row among them. Molly Brown was the only one who wanted to go back. Three years later, she walked the picket line at Ludlow. She never gave up on her fellow man."

Jo Anne got off the stool. Her face was inches from mine. "You were not thinking about Molly Brown or my paintings. Don't pretend you were."

"Pardon?"

"Don't lie, Aaron. Every thought you have is always on your face."

"I asked you to marry me. I never got an answer. Silence makes people think the worse."

Her eyes hazed over. "You thought I insulted God?"

"No, I did not think that."

"Then what did you think?"

"You're already spoken for. No man will replace your father."

Her face was like a sheet of white paper with nothing written on it. "That's the most invasive and arrogant statement anyone has ever said to me."

The phone rang. She picked up the receiver and placed it to her ear, her face dilated with anger. She handed the receiver to me. "It's for the ice cream guy," she said.

"WHAT'S COOKING, STONEY?"

"Bad haps, man." His voice was like fingernails on a blackboard. "They're gonna do it again. You gotta come get me."

"Who's going to do what again?"

"What they did to Moon Child."

"You got to spell it out, Stoney."

"They got a ceremony up in the rocks. It's dark even when the sun's out. You're not gonna believe it. I didn't because I was on acid. Acid is no good, man."

I could hear diesel engines huffing and airbrakes blowing in the background. "Tell me where you are."

"In the phone booth."

"Which phone booth? What's the closest town?"

"I don't know."

"What brand of gas do they sell there?"

"It's gas, ice cream guy. Fuck. My head hurts."

"Who's at the ceremony? Just give me one name."

"It's not one person. It's the devil. No. A bunch of them. All with the same face."

I felt my knees go weak. "Hang up and dial the operator. Tell her you're being kidnapped. Then leave the receiver off the hook and start running. Wave down a truck or a highway patrol."

He started to hiccup. "They're coming . . . They're coming . . . They . . . Oh, shit, ice cream guy. They're gonna punish me."

Someone opened the phone booth door and pulled the receiver from Stoney's hand. "Is this who I think it is?" a voice said.

"How's it hangin', Doyle? You like movies? Did you ever see *The Maltese Falcon*? Humphrey Bogart takes a pistol away from Sidney Greenstreet's bodyguard and throws it to Greenstreet and says something like, 'Here, a crippled newsie took it off him.' For some reason you make me think of that line."

"I'll be looking you up, Broussard. You don't know where I am. But I know where you are."

"Last time out, you didn't do too well," I said.

"You don't get it, do you?"

"Afraid not."

"You remember Cherry Alley in Tokyo? The signs out front said 'Fuckie-Suckie'? Why do you think we went to Jo Anne's house?"

"You're an evil man, Doyle."

"She can give good head, but that's about it. By the way, she said you're a lousy lay."

He hung up.

"JIMMY DOYLE GOT on the phone?" Jo Anne said.

"Yeah, he's got Stoney pretty scared," I said.

"What'd he say?"

"He's a jerk and not worth talking about. The issue is Stoney. I wonder if he's being used to set us up."

"He's bait?"

"Yeah," I said.

"What did Stoney tell you? You looked a little gray for a minute."

"He was talking about a ceremony that involved the devil."

"He has brain damage," she said. "Don't pay attention to what he says."

"I get the sense he's talking about human sacrifice."

"What?"

"I think I know where Stoney and Doyle are headed."

"You're thinking about going there?" she asked.

"Will you marry me, Jo Anne?"

"I love you. I can say that truthfully. But I can't handle all this crap."

"Maybe I shouldn't have asked."

She looked at the stove. "Your food's burning."

Chapter Twenty-Six

I DUMPED THE PAN in the trash, then tried to call Wade Benbow at home. No answer. I pulled on my coat.

"What are you doing?"

"Leaving."

"Just like that? It's been kicks?"

"I wish it had turned out different, Jo. Tell Spud and Cotton and Maisie I'm sorry I got them out on a bad night."

I went out the door. The snow crystals stung like chips of glass in the wind. I got into my car and began to back out of the driveway. The front door of the house flew open, and Jo Anne ran for the car in a sheepskin coat and a beat-up felt cowboy hat tied on with a scarf. She jumped into the passenger seat and slammed the door. "You're not going anywhere without me," she said.

"I have to do this on my own, Jo."

"Do you have a flashlight?"

"No."

She turned off the engine and pulled out the key. "Stay here."

She went back into the house and returned a few minutes later with a flashlight and a deerskin bag tied on her belt. The bag banged against the doorjamb when she got in.

"What's in there?" I said.

"Shit."

"Jo—"

She leaned forward so she could see the sky through the windshield. "The storm is coming right out of the Sangre de Cristos. The clouds look like they're full of coal dust or smoke from a big fire."

I CAUGHT THE TWO-LANE up to Ludlow, then turned west on the dirt road that led through the site of the massacre and the Cordova Pass and then northwest to the mountains named for the blood of Christ. The night was black and the snow white and blinding in my headlights, the wiper blades coated with ice. "What's that up ahead?" Jo Anne asked.

"The miners' shacks or what's left of them," I said.

"No, there's a man. I saw him."

"Out in this weather?"

"Hit your brights."

I clicked the floor switch. "Jesus!" I said.

I swerved to miss the figure who stood in the middle of the road, his hooded face as gray as bone. The front of the car hit a pothole and splashed water and mud all over the windshield. But I had no doubt who the figure was. I had seen him at the United Farm Workers gathering and had spoken with him outside the Lowry bunkhouse.

The engine had died. When I restarted it, the wipers went wild, then stopped for no reason, slush sliding in waves down the windshield. My heart was thudding, my breath short. "You know who that is?" I said.

"No."

"Think."

"I have no idea who he is."

"Did you see his eyes?" I asked.

"What about them?"

"They're black sockets. They're not eyes." I slowly accelerated. Ahead of us, lightning forked into the top of a mountain that penetrated the clouds. "I think he's the man called Bible-thumping Bob. I also think that's not his real name."

She peered into the whiteness of the snow swirling at us. "He's gone. How could anyone survive out here by himself?"

"Does he look like somebody you used to know?"

"Don't do this to me, Aaron."

"Tell the truth. Stop denying what we're seeing."

"I know the difference between the dead and the living. My father is dead."

"What was your father's first name?"

"Robert," she said, her mouth a tight line. "It was Robert."

"There's no possibility that's your dad?"

"I looked for him two years. Robert McDuffy is dead."

"I've talked with him, Jo."

She stared straight ahead, her brow furrowed. "I think this man is here to see you, not me, Aaron. Maybe it has to do with your friend who died in Korea."

"Saber was MIA."

"That's what I mean," she said. "Your friend is dead. He's not coming back. And neither is my father."

A bolt of lightning struck a huge tree not over thirty yards from us, splitting the trunk in a clean V all the way to the roots, turning every leaf on every branch into a tiny flame. I would have sworn I saw Moon Child standing by the tree, her face as expressionless as bread dough, her bangs and eyes jet black.

"What did you just see?" Jo Ann asked.

"Nothing," I said. "There's nothing out there. Shadows play tricks on you."

"Aaron?"

"What?"

"I can't say this."

"Can't say what?"

"Do you think this is hell?"

I WAS GUESSING AT the destination of Stoney and Jimmy Doyle and their friends. My friend at the Sally had mentioned Cordova Pass and the Sangre de Cristos, both in alpine country filled with peaks over eleven thousand feet high. The road I chose had no signs, no campgrounds, not even a Forest Service lookout tower. The road was six inches deep with mud and in some places eroded away, particularly on corners that overlooked thick stands of fir trees two hundred feet straight down. The only gifts the road offered were the deep, swerving tire marks of a very heavy, very large vehicle such as a school bus, and a four-foot-broad ornamental wood star that may have fallen off its roof.

"Look at the snowbank between those two Ponderosas," I said. "That's the star my friend at the Sally was talking about. He said Marvin had a star like that tied on top of the bus. German farmers in the Midwest call it a *hexe*. They think it will bring them good luck. They evidently don't know *hexe* in German means 'witch.'"

"Tell me what you saw when the lightning struck the tree."

"Moon Child," I replied.

"I saw her, too. I've never been this afraid. I'm just too tired to show it."

We went over a rise and around a pile of broken rocks that had rolled down the hill. We kept going until we were above the storm, at an elevation where the road was dry and the stars visible through the clouds. The road ended at a box canyon, its walls high and sheer, a reddish-brown color more like river clay than rock, forming a natural amphitheater.

The bus's tires were stenciled across the entrance into the canyon. I cut my engine and headlights. Somehow the engine flared to life again, then coughed and died.

"What's happening?" she said.

"Maybe the carburetor and a bad plug or two acting up."

"There's fires burning at the base of that cliff."

"You want to leave?"

"I don't know," she said. Her chest was rising and falling. She rubbed the backs of her hands as though they were chafed. "I really don't know."

"We can go back to town and tell Wade Benbow what we saw."

"Tell him we saw what? A murdered girl and a man with no eyes?"

"No one knows where we are, Jo."

"I Scotch-taped a note for Spud and Cotton and the Japanese woman inside the little window on the front door."

"Do you have my gun in your bag?"

"Yeah. I bought some shells for it, too. It's not going to do us any good here, though." She paused. "Is it?"

"We both saw the hooded man and Moon Child. That means that nothing we thought we knew about the world is true. It's like starting our lives all over. How many people get to do that?"

"I bet the dead think it's a great opportunity," she said. "Except they can't tell us that because their mouths and eyes are stopped with dirt. I want to get this over with. Good God, do I want to get this over with."

Chapter Twenty-Seven

I HATE VIOLENCE. I hated it then; I hate it now. I hate even more the people who flaunt it and take pleasure in speaking of it. They belong to a culture of cowards and misogynists who have chewing tobacco for brains and never make the connection between their obsession with firearms and carnality, penis envy and white supremacy. It's not their fault; most of them were unwanted at birth. Every one of them is cruel, every one of them a spiritual failure. The louder their rhetoric, the more craven their behavior. I have entertained thoughts about them that make me ashamed, because in some ways they are more victim than perpetrators.

The Holland family wrote their history in blood. My father, James Eustache Broussard, went to war but was not like the Hollands. I never heard him utter an unkind or profane word, not once. He wore a formal coat at the table even when he ate alone. He also went over the top five times at the Somme and would leave the room when others spoke of war.

When I was small and asked him why he shunned the subject, he said, "Hell is more than half of paradise, Aaron. So we should take no joy in the destruction of the Eden that was given us." That's how I discovered the work of Edwin Arlington Robinson.

I mentioned Nathaniel Hawthorne and Goodman Brown

earlier. Goodman wandered into the New England darkness and on the trail met a figure who walked with a cane carved in the likeness of a serpent, so realistic it seemed to ripple in the figure's grip. But rather than flee the figure's presence, Goodman convinced himself he was above temptation and need not fear the guile of a demonic spirit. As a result, his faith in man and God was robbed from him.

I wondered if I was about to take the same journey, although I seemed to have no alternative. I had to save Stoney. I also had to save my own sanity and confront the man who had no eyes. I had another motivation. (And this is where my pride got to me.) Was I being offered the chance to step through the curtain? Allowed to unravel the great mysteries? Allowed to see my best friend, Saber Bledsoe, and ask his forgiveness?

My father, who was buried alive under an artillery barrage on the Somme River, said there was no such thing as death. We enter eternity at birth, he said, and at a certain time in our journey, we go deeper into a meadow that is sprinkled with flowers and grazed by herbivores, where there are no fences and where we turn our swords into plowshares and like the earth abideth forever.

That's what he learned inside his premature burial place, one that stank of cordite and mustard gas.

With these thoughts in mind, I parked the car in a dark spot by the side of the mountain, removed a pair of binoculars from the glove box, and, with Jo Anne at my side, walked into the box canyon.

IMMEDIATELY INSIDE ITS parameters, the temperature changed dramatically, as though we had entered another dimension, perhaps caused by a weather inversion that had sealed the canyon, creating a bubble of warm air that had molded itself against the rocks and trapped the firelight on the cliffs and subsumed the smell of woodsmoke and burnt sage and the pine needles under our feet.

I put the binoculars to my eyes. The scene was idyllic. How could evil exist in a natural environment unmarked by the Industrial Age? Then I saw the bus parked below a row of giant boulders at the far end of the canyon. It looked like a toy, a harmless artifact borrowed from the culture of *The Saturday Evening Post*.

"Do you see any people?" Jo Anne asked.

"There's smoke coming from behind those boulders, but I can't see anyone."

I handed her the binoculars. She fitted them to her eyes and adjusted the focus. Then she wiped her eyes and looked through them again.

"What is it?" I said.

"Turkey buzzards flying in and out of the smoke. But they're too big."

"What's too big?"

"What I saw," she said. "They were as big as people."

I took back the binoculars. "There's a big gush of black smoke rising from between two of the boulders. Is that what you saw?"

"No, it didn't look like smoke at all."

We were on a narrow deer trail about a third of the way to the bus when we heard the dry, clattering sound of slag or small rocks above us. Jo Anne looked up, then grabbed my arm.

"Oh, Aaron!" she said. "Oh my God, Aaron!"

"What?" I said, off balance from her pressure on my arm.

"On that ledge." She fumbled in her bag for the gun, then dropped it. She looked up again. "Oh, God! Oh, God! Oh, God!"

Now I could see them, four or five of them, going from rock to rock. They looked like stick figures, similar in structure to a praying mantis but as tall as human beings. They bounded away as fast as they had come.

"You saw that, didn't you?" she said.

"Yes," I replied.

"What are they?" she said. I could hear her breathing when I didn't answer.

"I don't know what they are."

She picked up the .38 and tried to give it to me. "I never shot a gun."

"I don't want it," I said.

"You're suddenly a pacifist? While we die here?"

I saw the look on her face and didn't argue. "There's an answer to this, but we'll find it elsewhere. Start walking toward the entrance. Don't look back. If anything happens to me, keep going."

Minutes later, I saw sparks spiraling into the air just outside the canyon, followed by a great red, black, and yellow ball of flame rising from the windows and roof of my car. The stick figures had formed a chain across the canyon's entrance.

Chapter Twenty-Eight

I COULD SEE NO way out except up. If we kept going and stayed in the shadows, eventually we would find another deer trail, one that could take us to a cliff or a place where we could get over the lip of the canyon. The problem was the stick figures we had seen in the rocks. What were they? I knew there was no rational explanation for what we had seen. Please don't misunderstand. I have never been keen on the physical sciences, because most of them usually end in a cul-de-sac. Einstein believed that parallel lines intersect on the edges of infinity. Try to visualize that and see what it does to your head. If the physical sciences don't always slide down the pipe, who can say the stick figures were not real?

We worked our way along the canyon wall, the trail smooth and clean and worn from the passage of both hoofed and foot padded animals, the stone cool to the touch. The boulders around us were enormous and shielded us from view of the people in the bus or those who had built the fires. Jo Anne was in front of me, pausing at each bend in the trail before continuing on. I could see stars through the trees that rimmed the canyon. There was a dry wash twenty yards ahead of us, slanted at forty degrees. With luck, it would put us on a ledge where we could stay until sunrise, when the nightmare world we had stumbled into would recede like a harmless shadow.

"Jo," I whispered.

She turned around, then stepped into a hole, twisting her ankle, her mouth opening silently, her face draining. I grabbed her before she could fall and lowered her to the ground. "I think I tore it," she said.

I cupped my hand on her ankle. It was already hot. "Hang on," I said. I worked her back against a boulder so she could sit up comfortably and keep her ankle straight out and the other leg pulled up. I took off my coat and put it behind her head.

"Go on, get out of here," she said.

"That won't happen."

"That's what you told me to do if you got hurt."

"I learned long ago not to take my own advice."

"We need help, Aaron."

"I'm not leaving you."

"God, you're stubborn. I want to pound you with my fists."

I looked around us. "This isn't a bad place to be. They can't see us. We have the gun. It could be worse."

"You have to go for help."

"Out here, there is no help." I sat down and put my arm around her. "Let's rest a little while. Cotton and Spud and Maisie know we're here."

"What time is it?"

I looked at my watch. Then tapped on the glass.

"It stopped?" she said.

"I must have knocked it against a rock."

But Jo Anne was not one you put the slide on. "What time did it stop?"

"Exactly midnight. Even the second hand is straight up."

Had we stepped out of time? I had no idea. The shadow of a large object raced across the boulders around us. I tried to get my binoculars on it, but it was moving too fast. Then I smelled a stench that was unmistakable, one that makes you gag, one that you associate with a rendering plant or hair burning, one that could have come from the stacks in Poland during World War II.

Jo Anne choked as though she had swallowed a fish bone. "What are they doing out there?"

"Who knows?"

"Tell me."

"I'm going to take the binoculars down the trail. Here's the gun. I'll be right back."

"Aaron, I don't want these people or creatures or whatever they are to get their hands on me. Understand what I'm saying?"

"Yeah, but it's not going to come to that," I said.

"Lose the charade and promise you won't let them get me, Aaron," she said.

"I won't let them get you, Jo Anne."

I WALKED BEHIND THE boulders along the deer trail to a spot where I could see the bus and the people who had gathered at the head of the canyon. I focused the binoculars on a table rock that seemed to serve as an altar. A bonfire was burning on it, and Mr. and Mrs. Lowry were standing up the slope from it, the firelight flickering on their faces. She wore a black ankle-length dress with a white lace collar similar to the one worn by the wife of Rueben Vickers. Mr. Lowry was also dressed in black and wearing a wide-brimmed, tall-crowned hat that had a silver buckle on its band, as either a Puritan or a French musketeer might wear.

Below them, on the other side of the bonfire, were Lindsey

Lou and Orchid and Jimmy Doyle and Marvin Fogel and people I had never seen. They all seemed to be waiting on something or someone, perhaps the creatures flying over the canyon, maybe an entity that had more power than all of them together.

I shifted the glasses and was suddenly looking at the faces of Cotton Williams and Spud Caudill and Maisie, who was probably the only woman in the world who had ever believed in Spud. I stepped backward, behind the boulder, unable to accept what I had just seen. Maisie and Spud and Cotton had become acolytes in a demonic cult?

I closed my eyes and tried to think, then realized that something was wrong, that the body language of my friends was out of sync with that of the people around them, their expressions wan and resentful. I looked again through the glasses. Cotton had a rope around his neck; Spud's fedora was gone; Maisie's scarf was knotted around her mouth; all of them had their wrists tied behind them.

Then I saw the birds that Jo Anne had seen, except they weren't birds, nor were they witches on brooms. They had faces like bats and wings that were singed and streamed ashes. A stick figure leaped back and forth across the bonfire, then skittered up into the rocks. But none of this explained the odor that was like incinerated offal.

I lifted the glasses again and focused them on the bonfire. I did not believe what I was looking at. It was too cruel to be real. The humped and charred remains of a human being, wrists bound in back, head slumped, was in the center of the flames. The victim was slight of build, with arms that could have been pipe cleaners. Stoney? Was there not one person who would try to protect this innocent kid? I thought I had seen the worst in human beings in Korea, and I mean our F-86s strafing miles of civilian refugees as they fled south on foot, hoping for safe harbor. I looked at the fire and wanted to weep. No, I wanted to kill the people who had done this.

I went back down the trail to Jo Anne and squatted beside her.

"What did you see?" she asked.

"Mr. and Mrs. Lowry seem to be in charge."

"That's crazy."

"They're dressed like people from the seventeenth century."

"Who else is down there?"

"Cotton and Maisie and Spud. Their hands are tied."

"They were our only hope," she said.

"I've got to tell you something else. Someone was burned to death in that bonfire. I think these bastards killed Stoney."

"No, no, don't say that."

"I know what I saw. It could be someone else. But they burned somebody alive."

"The Lowrys are doing this?" she said. "This is madness, Aaron. No, this is hell. We found it on earth. It's not a myth."

"We need to get to the top of the canyon," I said. "There's no other way out. Are you up to it?" I tried to smile.

"Whatever it takes. Who else was down there?"

"Orchid and Lindsey Lou, Jimmy Doyle and Marvin Fogel."

"Moon Child was their friend."

"Orchid and Lindsey Lou are scared. Doyle and Fogel are butt crust."

"The Lowrys are actually behind all this? The people who had us to dinner? The man you compared to your father?"

"I told you what I saw."

"There's something wrong in that picture," she said. "The Lowrys? That doesn't make sense."

"We'd better get going. There's only one trail that goes to the top. It's awful steep. There's not much cover on it, either."

"They can see us?"

"If we let them," I replied.

I GOT HER TO her feet, and we began walking up the trail, then branched off to another trail that led to a cave. The opening was probably less than thirty yards below the canyon's rim. The pain in Jo Anne's ankle was obvious. I tried carrying her but tripped and almost dropped her.

"Set me down," she said.

"No, I think we can make it."

"We'll be out in the open. Those creatures flying in the air will see us. Get help and come back. I'll stay in the cave."

I eased her down on a smooth claylike spot fifteen feet from the cave's entrance, then put the binoculars on the bonfire. The number of people gathered before it had doubled. They were cheering and clapping. I moved the glasses back to Mr. and Mrs. Lowry. Again, I could not believe what I was watching. Rueben and Darrel Vickers were standing next to the Lowrys. Both father and son were wearing black robes with red trim, although Darrel wore his coned-up cowboy straw hat as well. A German Luger hung from Darrel's right hand. He must have told a joke, because the crowd was laughing. However, the faces of the Lowrys were shiny with fear, as though a gravitational shift in the earth had just occurred and they were the only ones who would be affected by it.

Then Darrel Vickers pointed the Luger's barrel at the side of Mr. Lowry's head and fired two shots, *pop-pop*, that fast, like a fool having fun at a funeral. Mr. Lowry dropped straight down, stone dead before he hit the ground.

I lowered the binoculars, stupefied. Jo Anne looked up at me. "Those sounded like gunshots," she said.

"Darrel Vickers just murdered Jude Lowry."

"*What?*"

"He killed him with a German Luger. His father is with him."

"What about Mrs. Lowry?"

I put the binoculars to my eyes. "She's just standing there. I think she's crying."

"What about your friends, Spud and—"

"The crowd's pushing them toward the fire."

"We can't leave them, Aaron."

I could hear the wind blowing in the pines on the lip of the canyon; I could smell the odor of stone and cave air and hard-packed damp clay and bat guano and the salty smell of birds' nests. I thought of a womb and the symbolism of Elijah finding the voice of God inside a cave. I do not mean that a miracle had been prepared for me. But I do believe that terror can rip away the curtain that binds us to all the mundane distractions of the world and also the lies of kings and dictators and militarists and those who would turn the Grand Canyon into a gravel pit if they had the opportunity.

I looked at my watch, although I cannot explain why. It had started ticking again. The second hand indicated the time was five seconds past midnight, as though my life were being reset or I had stepped into an alternate reality, one where my blackouts had taken me many times.

I heard a voice that Jo Anne did not hear. More important, I saw a man she did not see. He was standing inside the cave, unshaved, wearing fatigues that were sweat-stained and dirty, his skin powdered with dust, his dog tags and a P-38 can opener hanging on a chain outside his shirt. He was grinning.

Saber? I said.

The one and only.

Are you dead?

Kind of. Things aren't too orderly on this side of the Big Divide. I keep thinking I might wake up at battalion aid.

The flamethrowers didn't—

No, you were carrying me. A 105 came in short. Lights out. Your gal looks like Esther Williams. Does she have a sister?

How can we get out of this, Saber?

Leave your probs to the Bledsoe. I got something for you.

He went deeper into the cave. I looked over my shoulder at Jo Anne. She was motionless, frozen in time, her gaze fixed on nothing. Saber returned, cradling an object with both palms. *Catch!*

It was an M1. I caught it with both hands. He draped a cloth bandolier stuffed with .30-06 clips across the bolt.

We're outnumbered, Saber.

Not with that.

It just moved. In my hand.

Time to stomp ass and take names, Aaron. Your friends are depending on you.

Are you coming back, Saber?

Wish I knew. Remember when we drag-raced on the edge of the surf down at Galveston? The salt ate the floor out of my '39 Ford. Why'd I get dead, Aaron?

I wish neither one of us went to Korea.

You gotta do something for kicks. Keep a cool stool. You heard it first from the Bledsoe himself.

Suddenly, he was gone and I was wide awake, the stars as white and cold as dry ice above the canyon, the pines swelling in the wind. The hands on my watch had stopped again. Jo Anne was looking up at me.

I knelt beside her and placed her fingers on the M1's stock. "Feel that?" I said.

"Yes."

"My best friend burned his initials there in the spring of 1953."

Down below, people were shouting, their voices filled with hate and bloodlust and a form of desire that cannot be sated, cannot be explained, and I am convinced is passed down by a single creature who, millions of years ago, cracked apart his shell and was startled to discover the feast that awaited him.

Chapter Twenty-Nine

If you subscribe to a Judeo-Christian view of our tenure on earth, war does not leave you with many positive memories. There is a short-lived exception, though. For days before you're moved into the line, you carry a nauseating ball of fear in your stomach and a stench in your armpits like spoiled clams. Then you hear a sound on your flank similar to Chinese firecrackers popping; in seconds it grows in volume and velocity until it becomes a sustained roar of automatic weapons and mortar and bazooka rounds and hand grenades and incoming artillery and explosions like locomotive engines blowing apart and dirt showering down on your steel pot, followed by the screams of those whose arms or legs are gone and whose torsos twitch on the ground as though electrocuted.

Then it stops in the same way it started. You slide down in your hole and touch yourself all over and, in disbelief, discover the Angel of Death has passed you by. The joy you experience is like none you have ever known. You've not only proved your courage, you're painted with magic, chosen by fate to survive the war and accomplish great deeds, to walk the earth as the friend of God and man.

Perhaps that same evening, in the twilight, you sit on the edge of your foxhole and eat your C rations, pork and beans or chopped eggs and ham, and listen to the dull knocking of

.50-caliber and watch the tracers glide like segments of neon into purple hills filled with enemies you no longer fear. The sense of peace and control you experience is ethereal.

Of course, you eventually learn all of this is an illusion, but like many self-manufactured opiates, it's a grand one just the same.

And that was how I felt after Saber gave me his M1. It was a beautiful weapon, with its heft and balance and peep sight and deadly accuracy and its eight-round clips you could load as fast as you could thumb one into the magazine and roll the heel of your hand off the bolt.

I looked down at the bonfire. Maisie and Spud and Cotton had been pushed on their knees.

"What are you going to do?" Jo Anne said.

"This," I replied.

I propped myself against a boulder and aimed at Darrel Vickers's back and fired a solitary round. The report echoed through the entirety of the canyon. I saw him grab the top of his left shoulder with his right hand and look at the blood on it. The crowd receded from the bonfire like water running backward. Some ran for the bus; others crouched among the shadows in the rocks. Both Darrel and his father looked up the incline in my direction, although I doubted they could see me. Mrs. Lowry was bent into a ball over her husband's body, her face buried in his chest.

"That you, Broussard?" Darrel yelled. "You can't shoot for shit!" He waited in the silence. "No comment? Is Jo Anne there? Jimmy Doyle says she chugs serious pud."

I aimed through the peep sight again, this time lower, right under the breastbone. I wet my lip and began to squeeze the trigger.

Darrel cupped his hands around his mouth, seemingly indifferent to the round he might have to eat. "Think you got us by the shorts? Watch your army buddy at work!"

Doyle came out of the shadows and stood behind Spud and Maisie and Cotton with a cigarette lighter raised above his head.

"Your friends are soaked in gasoline!" Darrel said. "Come down or we light them up!"

I saw a shadow zoom across the rocks around us. I looked up and saw one of the winged creatures making a wide turn, coming back for another flyover.

I wanted to burn the whole clip on Darrel. I thirsted to shed his blood in every way I could. I knew then I had denied my true identity my whole life, that indeed the Holland legacy of violence and mayhem had always lived inside me. I wanted to blow Darrel Vickers apart one piece at a time, then reload as I walked down the slope and do the same to his father. I wanted to kill them for the boy whose blackened body was little more than embers about to collapse into ash, and I wanted to kill them for Moon Child and all the other people they had tortured and murdered, and I knew, like my ancestors, I would never have a minute's remorse.

Jo Anne got to her feet and put her hand on my shoulder "What should we do?" she asked.

"About what?"

"Everything."

"Stay behind me," I said.

I began firing at Jimmy Doyle. I saw his face and head break apart like a flowerpot. I saw one round drill through his throat and another cut the fingers that gripped his lighter. Then I swung the iron sights on Darrel and got off one wide round before he went behind some rocks and began firing wildly with the Luger. I also fired at his father, then the bolt locked open, and the spent shell and the empty clip ejected with the brief me-tallic *clink* that every soldier who has fired the M1 rifle never forgets.

DARREL WAS RUNNING up the slope, headed for cover in the larger rocks. I pushed another clip into the magazine and released the bolt and fired three rounds, each ricocheting and whining into the darkness with a sound like a bobby pin twanging.

"I've got to get a better shot at Darrel."

"You're going?"

"Not far."

"Stay."

"We have to put Darrel out of business."

"Please stay."

"I'll be back."

I walked down a path to the edge of the clearing, my head roaring with sound, hating to leave Jo Anne, wondering if I was making a terrible mistake.

"Hey, ice cream guy. It's me," I heard a voice say. Stoney stepped into the light. He wore a mackinaw and a battered football helmet and navy blue sweatpants and pink tennis shoes. "Is that Jimmy Doyle? Geez, what a mess. His face looks like a pepperoni pizza that got run over by a garbage truck."

"I thought that was you in the bonfire," I said.

"Oh, no, he was a hitchhiker. They were really mean to him, ice cream guy. Just because he got into their stash."

I was trying to look at everyone in the clearing, including Maisie and Spud and Cotton, and listen to Stoney at the same time. Also I was drunk on adrenaline from having just killed a man. "What stash?" I said.

"Bags and bags of it. Behind the panels on the sides of the bus. The kid was sucking it up his nose like an anteater."

"Do you know where Darrel Vickers's father went?"

"The guy with the face like a bowl full of walnuts?"

If Stoney ever got off chemicals, I was determined to get him into a creative writing class. "Yeah, that guy."

"Stay away from him. That guy is definitely a criminal."

"*He's* a criminal?"

"Fucking A, I know his type. I wouldn't trust him."

I took out my long-blade Swiss Army knife. "Cut my friends loose, will you? I need to get Jo Anne."

"What for?" he said.

"To get out of here?"

"She's not going anywhere, ice cream guy. This is the Shitsville where bad people go. Nobody told you?"

I RAN UP A trail, the M1 gripped with both hands at forty-five degrees, my lungs aching in the thin air, and tried to think my way through all the events of the last two hours. Nothing made sense. I was surrounded by sandstone boulders, some with petroglyphs carved on them. A Comanche moon, huge and yellow, the kind you associate with summer rather than fall, had risen above the canyon. I had just killed one man and had tried to kill another and felt no regret. I had watched the execution of Mr. Lowry, a man I believed to be a genteel farmer and egalitarian patriot, and now, if I had the chance, I was going to cap both Darrel and Rueben Vickers and any others of their ilk I could lay my peep sight on.

But inside this giant grotesque web hung with bat-faced winged creatures, probably from the Abyss, I had returned to the worst day of my life, the one I denied on a daily basis, the day my best friend died at Pork Chop Hill or, worse, was captured and sent across the Yalu to be used as a lab rat.

I have always been a believer. I don't care what the naysayers and cynics say. In fact, I say fuck them. The big blue marble, the constellations, the Milky Way, the wine-dark waves of the ancient Greeks are filled with magic and with us forever.

I knew now that Saber would always be with me. Just like the days we drifted in his hot rod down South Main in Houston, down by Rice University, under the live oaks and Spanish moss and in the drive-in hangouts, the throaty roar of his twin Hollywood mufflers rumbling on the asphalt, convertibles full of pretty girls waving as they flew past us, Jackie Brenston and Gatemouth Brown blaring from the radio.

So I would not fear whatever happened that night in a box canyon that somehow had become a twisted mirror of the America I loved and fought for. As Stephen Crane wrote at the close of *The Red Badge of Courage*, the great death was only the great death, not to be sought, not to be feared, but treated as an inconsequential player in the human comedy.

I was breathing heavily when I reached the plateau that led to the place I had left Jo Anne. I had five rounds in the clip and many more in the bandolier. My heart was beating triumphantly, the way it had when Saber and I survived our first day of combat. I knew that Saber and I would prevail again, that the evil forces of the world were essentially craven and not worth grieving on. Up the trail I thought I saw Rueben Vickers. I could have shot him, but I felt pity rather than hatred toward him, an angry man who knew his seed should have been cast upon the ground.

Then I rounded a corner and looked into the faces of Rueben Vickers, Henri Devos, and Jo Anne. Henri was standing next to Jo Anne, his arm around her waist, his face gleeful. Darrel stepped from behind a rock and pressed the muzzle of his Luger behind my ear. "Let the rifle fall to the ground, asshole," he said.

"Jo?" I said.

She didn't answer.

"You want your brains on her shirt?" Darrel said.

I let the M1 drop. He peeled the bandolier off my waist. "Jo?" I repeated.

"How does it feel, former instructor at the University of Southwestern Louisiana?" Henri said. He wore an electric-blue backpack and lugged boots and hiking knickers with white socks pulled up on his shins.

"Jo, say something."

"What's to say?" she replied. "You never listen. That's always been our problem, you just never get it."

Chapter Thirty

"Pick up the Garand," Mr. Vickers said. "I'll carry the Luger."

"It's called an M1," Darrel said.

"I was in the army," his father said. "I know what it's called."

"Okay, *Dad*."

Darrel told me to stand back, then handed the Luger to his father. He leaned over to pick up Saber's rifle. Then he hesitated, staring down at it.

"What are you waiting on?" Mr. Vickers said.

"It moved."

"It did what?"

Darrel put one hand on the stock, then jumped back. "It came alive. Just like a snake."

His father shook his head. He slapped his son on the ear with the flat of his hand, then gave him the Luger and picked up the M1 and balanced it on his shoulder. "I don't know how I got involved with you pissants. I really don't."

Darrel stood stiff as a post as he watched his father walk down the trail.

I walked ahead of them down the trail, numb and sick at heart at Jo Anne's behavior.

Most of the bus community, which was far more numerous than the original group, had stayed in the shadows, leaderless and without direction, their expressions disjointed, as though their messiah had deserted them and they did not know who they were or why they were there. I could smell weed and see a kid shooting up with an eyedropper. A half-dozen girls dressed in white had clasped hands and were dancing barefoot in a circle, stoned out of their heads.

Jimmy Doyle's body still lay curled on its side, like a broken worm. Mrs. Lowry had disappeared. Marvin Fogel was flinging logs on the bonfire, crushing the remains of the burned hitchhiker, as though the intensity of his work would extricate him from the chaos taking place around him.

Stoney was nowhere in sight. Neither were Spud and Cotton and Maisie. The tape that had bound their wrists lay on the ground.

"Looks like your friends bagged ass," Darrel said.

I looked over my shoulder. Henri was walking slowly behind us, his right arm locked around Jo Anne. She refused to look at me.

"How's it feel to get sold out?" Darrel said.

I didn't reply.

"She's a prick-teaser, man," he said. "That's why I dumped her."

"*You* dumped her?"

"After I fucked her brains out."

"Don't use that language, Darrel," Mr. Vickers said.

"Your son smeared his feces all over Jo Anne's house," I said.

"He did what?"

"That's the way a succubus operates," I said. "It probably has something to do with toilet training."

"Darrel?" Mr. Vickers said.

"He's lying, Daddy."

"Darrel has done things like this before, hasn't he?" I said.

Mr. Vickers knotted my shirt in his fist. "I'll break your teeth."

"You're a smart man, Mr. Vickers. How did you get mixed up with drug traffickers?"

He tightened his grip on my shirt. "I don't have anything to do with drugs."

"You want your son putting dope in his arm?"

He hit me in the mouth. I felt the blow all the way to my knees; the inside of my mouth tasted like pennies. I spat in the dirt. "You can tear me up, Mr. Vickers, but your son will always remain a coward. That's because of you, sir, not a succubus. Early on, you made him hate himself. That's why he suffocated the little girl in the refrigerator."

"Shut him up, Daddy," Darrel said.

"I was good to him," Mr. Vickers said. "I loved him. His mother tried to baby him. I made him a man."

"Is that the way he sees it?" I asked.

Mr. Vickers looked at his son. "Tell him, Darrel."

"Tell him what?"

"I loved you. I took care of you. I was proud of you."

"That's a tough sale, *Dads*. You made me cut my own switch."

"I did not."

"I was four or five the first time. I had on short pants. You whipped my legs until they were red all over. You knew how to do it, *Dads*."

"That's a goddamn lie," Mr. Vickers said. His face twitched violently, his right shoulder shaking.

"That M1 on your shoulder acting up, *Dads*?" Darrel said.

"I don't know what it's doing," Mr. Vickers said. "Here, I don't want the rifle."

"Does it feel like it's alive?" Darrel said.

"Take it."

"When I told you it was alive, you made fun of me."

Mr. Vickers swallowed, then pushed the rifle off his shoulder as though it were attached to his skin. When it hit the ground, he stepped away from it.

"Do you know why I shot Mr. Lowry, Daddy?" Darrel said.

"You said you were taking over. Maybe I don't agree with you shooting Jude, but he could be a difficult man. That was your choice, and I respect it."

"I lied. I was practicing. I'll show you."

Darrel lifted the Luger and fired a round into the center of his father's forehead. The muscles in Mr. Vickers's face collapsed or, better said, dissolved into tapioca, as though someone had whispered a dirty secret in his ear. The crowd in the shadows went silent and turned in unison, their features shiny and ghoulish as plastic masks, the eyes and mouths scooped by a spoon. The only sound was the wind. Darrel stared at the body. A dust devil spun through rocks, then lifted into the air and fell apart. "Bet you didn't think I could pop my old man, did you?" Darrel said to me.

"I feel sorry for you," I said.

"Why?" he said.

"You only get one father. I think he was telling you the truth."

"About what?"

"He loved you."

The change in his eyes was one I didn't expect. I think, for the first time in his life, Darrel understood the irrevocable nature of loss.

I WON'T BE FANCIFUL with you about death. It's a motherfucker no matter how you cut it, and needless to say, a violent death is worse. You don't have to go to war to find it, either. I saw a blowout on an offshore drilling rig that was the equal of any napalm bombing. The rig began to quiver, then the bolts started popping loose around the wellhead, and the casing jettisoned out of the hole and was clanging in the rigging like a junkyard falling down stairs, followed by a torrent of oil and gas and sludge that suddenly ignited and blew flame through the derrick and wilted the steel spars like licorice. Fourteen men died on the deck; the man racking pipe high up on the monkey board never knew what hit him.

I was on an offshore seismograph rig in '57 when Hurricane Audrey hit the Louisiana coast at 145 miles an hour, except we rode it out, even though we were loaded with canned dynamite and nitro caps. I don't think I was ever more frightened, before or since. Many people in Cameron Parish were drowned, and for minimum wage, I helped extract the dead from the swamp with grappling hooks and pull them out of trees. I remember how the dead all smelled like Clorox when you dragged them over the gunwale and into the boat.

I do not mean to assault anyone's sensibilities, but once you face death or reach out and touch it with your hand, or look into the half-lidded eyes of a woman or child or man whose life has been violently taken, you bond with them and silently try to console them for the theft of their lives. You promise to carry them in your heart and never tell anyone about it. I think that's what humanity is about.

Why do I talk about these things? I do not want the reader to mourn the fate of any character in this tale. Saber was brave and did not want me to mourn his death. That alone was gift enough for me. Since that night in the box canyon, I have never feared death, nor do I brood upon it. I'll take it a step further. Since that night, I have never feared anything in this world or the next.

---

230   JAMES LEE BURKE

WE WERE ALMOST to the bus. Henri was now holding Darrel's Luger. I kept trying to make Jo Anne look at me, with no success. My mind was tired, my body weak, my spiritual resources used up. Why would she not look at me? Had she actually betrayed me? *Think*, I told myself. What was I not seeing?

The .38 Police Special.

Her bag was still hanging on her waist.

"I want you to take a look inside the bus," Henri said. "I think you'll be pleasantly surprised."

I stepped up into the vestibule of the bus. Henri and Jo Anne followed me. Henri pulled off his backpack and dropped it heavily on the floor. Young people were eating take-out pizza and smoking dope. Lindsey Lou and Orchid were huddled behind a table stacked with tape-wrapped packages that probably contained cocaine or Mexican skag. Lindsey Lou and Orchid couldn't bring themselves to look at me.

"How you doin', girls?" I said. Both of them hung their heads. "This isn't your fault," I told them. "You got taken in by a bunch of shitheads."

"Don't test the envelope, Broussard," Henri said.

"What did you want to show me?" I said.

He pulled down a blanket that was draped on a clothesline. Behind it, Jo Anne's paintings were propped either against or all over a stuffed couch. The first one I saw clearly was of the children trapped inside the flames at the Ludlow Massacre.

"What do you think about that, Jo Anne?" Henri said.

"Thank you," she replied.

"You took them out of Jo Anne's house?" I said.

"No, Darrel did. But I got them back."

"Are you going to believe this guy?" I said to Jo.

She didn't answer. Her eyes were flat, her fingernails curled into her palms.

"You don't seem fazed too much by all this, Broussard," Henri said.

"What's to say? You win, I lose," I replied. Through a window, I could see Darrel among his newly acquired followers. He was still wearing his straw cowboy hat. "Here's the rub, Henri. You're stuck with who you are. And you're stuck with Darrel. Have fun with that."

"You don't have any questions about any of this or how it happened?" he said.

"It's the other way around, pal. I've always believed in the unseen world. It's you who's just waking up to it. The problem is you're on the wrong side, and in this case that makes you the dumbest academic I've ever met."

He was a vain man. I saw him fight with the insult, saw it seep into his face, his smile turn to a twitch, his gaze shift to Jo Anne, then back to me.

"Let's walk outside, Broussard," he said. "I've got something special planned for you."

"My friends Spud and Cotton and Maisie get loose on you?" I said.

"What about them?"

"My friend Cotton is a former Army Ranger and a mean motor scooter. He wiped out a bunch of SS under Vatican Square. Spud went up the road in Kentucky. His patron saint is Devil Anse Hatfield."

"I'm shaking."

Darrel stepped up on the vestibule. "What are you doing in here?"

"Looking at Jo Anne's canvases," Henri said.

"Get out here. Bring that asshole with you. We need to wrap this up."

In the blink while Darrel had distracted Henri, Jo Anne

pressed her foot on mine, looked directly into my eyes, then glanced at the electric-blue backpack Henri had dropped on the floor. She had gotten the .38 into his pack in case someone searched her drawstring bag. She had outthought Henri and Darrel from the jump, and she had also outthought me. But at that moment, the confirmation she had not betrayed me was worth far more to me than life itself.

Chapter Thirty-One

We LEFT THE bus. In the short time we were inside, the sky had turned black, smudging out the stars as though cannon smoke had drifted across them. Flashes of electricity were rolling through the clouds directly above the canyon, lighting the cliffs and the trees that grew between the rocks. The air was cold and sweet with the smell of rain. Marvin was still flinging logs on the bonfire, his face sweaty, the back of his coat split, his commitment to his task unflagging. He grinned at me and shrugged as if he had no choice in the matter.

"I've heard if you keep your eyes shut, your sensory system shuts down and the smoke does the rest," Henri said. "That's as good as I can offer."

Somebody pulled my arms behind me and taped my wrists. Lightning struck the canyon's rim, peeling back the darkness with a huge ball of yellow fire.

"Did you see that?" Darrel said.

"See what?" Henri said.

"A guy up on the cliff. Wearing black, with a hood."

"It could have been a dead tree."

"It was Bible-thumping-Bob," Darrel said. "What's he doing here?"

"Let's get this over with, Darrel. I want to get my old life back. Start over with Jo Anne," Henri said.

"Got news for you," Darrel said. "We need to tie up some loose ends. Starting with Miz Lowry. Time for you to get wet."

"That's on you," Henri said. "You took out her husband when you didn't have to. Clean up your own mess."

"I don't like your tone," Darrel said.

I felt raindrops strike my skin like drops of lead. I looked up at the sky and closed my eyes and let the rain slide down my face. I longed to have the M1 in my hands again. "Can I ask you guys something?"

"What, wisenheimer?" Darrel said.

"The kid you burned to death? You did it just because he got into your stash?"

"Yeah, an object lesson," Darrel replied.

"How old was he?"

"How should I know?" he said. "That's not your business, anyway." He kicked me behind the knee and sent me tumbling to the ground.

I had to help Jo Anne get to Henri's backpack, but I didn't know how.

"I don't want to watch this, Henri," she said.

"Then don't watch it," Darrel said.

She sniffed and rubbed her nose with her hand. "I'm coming down with a cold."

"Will you get her out of here?" Darrel said to Henri.

The sky lit up again. I thought I saw Spud and Cotton at the edge of the clearing. Darrel followed my line of sight. I was on my knees now. I started to stand. He took the Luger from Henri and chopped the butt down on my head. I felt like something had torn loose inside my skull. But I was on one knee now and still rising to my feet.

"Help me get him on the fire, Marvin!" Darrel said. "He's been the problem from the start! Grab his ankles!"

"I think we should talk this over," Marvin said. "I'm just the bus driver. I didn't do any of the killing here. No, sir, that's not my bag."

"You poured gasoline on that kid."

"I thought it was just to scare him."

"You want to take Broussard's place?"

"I think I'm going back to work at the Orange Julius in Portland. I was up for assistant manager."

Darrel knocked me to the ground again and went behind the bus and returned with a can of gasoline. He jerked the plug from the spout and showered gasoline on my head and face and clothes, then tossed the empty can in the fire. He watched the metal blacken and fold in on itself. Then he pointed the Luger at Henri. "Pick him up, Professor."

Henri lifted his hands, palms out, his eyes lowered, like a peacemaker. "This isn't the way to go, Darrel. Aaron is a smart guy. There're ways to work it out."

"I always knew you were a yellowbelly," Darrel said. He turned toward Jo Anne. "What are you looking at?"

"Nothing," she said.

"Bring me a can of Bud," he said.

I tried again to get to my feet, but Darrel placed his foot between my shoulder blades and shoved me down once more. I saw Jo Anne bend down over the backpack, then step off the vestibule. She pointed the .38 at Darrel with both hands, her arms straight out.

The kids on the bus followed her out. Those already outside had formed a huge semicircle around the clearing, their faces a study in shadow and firelight. They made me think of the children in Jo Anne's paintings.

"Put your pistol on the ground, Darrel," she said.

"I think I'll keep it," he replied.

"I'll have to shoot you."

"How about giving me some head before you do?"

I saw her trying to pull back the hammer. She had told me she knew nothing about guns. I believed her. Where were Spud and Cotton?

"Jo Anne, put your gun down," Henri said. "Darrel will kill you."

"Shut up, Henri," Darrel said. "This is between me and her." He worked a butane lighter out of his watch pocket. "I'm going to set Broussard on fire. What do you say to that, Jo Anne?"

She pulled the trigger. The hammer snapped on either an empty chamber or a dead round. She squeezed the trigger again. And again.

"I took the cartridges out," Darrel said. "You and Broussard are the perfect couple, Jo Anne. Complete losers. Gee, I wish I could have gone to college."

He walked toward me with the Luger swinging from his hand. I was on my knees. "Open your mouth," he said.

There was a collective moan in the crowd, as though a collective sin were being imposed upon them. Their behavior surprised even Darrel. They seemed to shrink individually in size, trying to hide inside themselves or inside one another. "Don't hurt ice cream guy!" Stoney called.

Then I saw him and Orchid and Lindsey Lou pick up stones and sticks. The others began to do the same. If they had possessed scythes and pitchforks and rakes, the scene would have been complete.

"What do you think you're doing?" Darrel said to them.

Out of the darkness, I saw Cotton Williams running toward Darrel, his shoulders humped, his silver hair streaming, his Buck knife open in his right hand. I never saw a man hit another man so hard with his body. Darrel looked like he had been broken in half, his robes torn open, his love handles and soft stomach exposed, the inside of his mouth as red as paint. Cotton pinned him to the ground with his knees, then inserted the point of his knife in Darrel's right nostril.

"Cotton—" I said.

Darrel's eyes were bulging. A broken tooth was glued to his chin.

"Cotton—" I said again.

"He felt up Maisie," Cotton said. "All over her. Same thing a guard did to her in one of those internment camps."

"Don't do it, Cotton," I said. "This isn't you."

"I killed my own son. What do you call that?"

I knew my words were to no avail. He was going to do it, and I couldn't blame him. Maybe I even wanted him to do it. Maybe we would all die that night. Maybe all of us had already entered eternity.

Maisie and Spud came out of the darkness. She placed her hand on Cotton's shoulder and knelt beside him, then leaned close to his ear. "You good man," she said. "You kind and brave, like Spud and Aaron. That why I love you. You give me knife now, Cotton." She took it gingerly from his hand.

I looked over my shoulder to see where Jo Anne was. But she was gone. And I mean gone

Epilogue

I woke in the morning by a railroad track miles away, with no memory of how I got there. My car was found by state foresters at the entrance to the box canyon. It had burned with such heat that the steering wheel had melted and all four tires had exploded. I told the cops I knew where several homicides had been committed. They found no evidence of any unusual events in the canyon and locked me in jail for two days because I was deemed a risk to myself.

I asked to see my friend Wade Benbow and was told he was out of town. I was released from jail and immediately went to Jo Anne's house. Her car was gone, her windows sealed with plywood. The hog farmer next door said he had no idea where she went. That night I got drunk and put back in the can, this time in a tank with a bunch of stewbums. While there, I had a surprise visitor and was allowed to speak with her in a conference room to which only lawyers normally had access.

"How are you, Aaron?" she said. "I'm so sorry to see you in bad straits."

"That's very good of you, Mrs. Lowry." I searched her face. She smiled pleasantly and seemed completely serene. I decided to turn the dial. "How is Mr. Lowry?"

"He's visiting his family in New England," she replied. She smelled as fresh as the morning dew.

"Do you know where Jo Anne McDuffy is?" I asked.

"Oh, the young girl you brought to dinner? No, I haven't seen her."

"How about Mr. Vickers? Is he out and about?"

"I wouldn't know. Mr. Lowry and I keep our distance from him. It's too bad about his son, though."

"Has Darrel been up to something?" I said.

"I guess you haven't heard. The Vickers boy and a college professor were found dead on a back road up by Ludlow. Their bodies were mangled. The police think that maybe a log truck ran over them. Are you sure you're all right, Aaron?"

"I'm fine. I sure wish I could get some news on Jo Anne, though."

"I'll let you know if I hear anything. I paid your bail. I also left an envelope with your wages and a little extra in it."

"I don't work for you anymore?"

"We're selling the farm. Your friends Spud and Maisie and Cotton have already moved on. They're starting up a poultry farm in New Mexico or Arizona, I think."

"Good for them," I said.

Mrs. Lowry got up to go. I was handcuffed to a chair by one wrist. She stroked my cheek with the ends of her fingers. I kept waiting for her to give up the ruse, but she didn't. "The door will always be open for you," she said, and winked. Then she bent over and blew her breath into my hair. "Sweet boy," she said. "Good enough to eat, that's what you are."

When I got out of the can the second time, I thumbed a ride to the Lowry farm, put my clothes and Smith Corona in a duffel bag and picked up my Gibson guitar and said goodbye to Chen Jen, then headed for the train yard outside Trinidad, hoping to grab a sidedoor Pullman that would take me to Albuquerque and on to a winter job working date palms around Calexico.

I might seem cavalier in my attitude toward the events I have described. However, I see it this way. I've acquired little knowledge and even less wisdom in my life, but early on, I learned not to argue with the world. I believed Jo Anne had chosen her father over me, and the two of them had gone on to a better life than the one I could have given her. I think her paintings went with her, too, and I believed that one day I would see them in a gallery or a museum.

I also learned that madness is madness, and we should not question its presence in the majority of the human race. And I learned, as George Orwell once said, that people are always better than we think they are. I was never a criminal, but I was in a southern prison when I was eighteen. A psychiatrist told me I suffered dissociative personality disorder; there were three different people sheltering inside my skin. I have had nonchemically induced blackouts all my life, and I have written and published forty books that I have trouble remembering, as though someone else wrote them. The characters in them are strangers and seem to have no origins; the words are like a rush of wind inside a cottonwood tree.

I do not dream any longer about the events in the box canyon. Even before I started to swing on a freight car for the screeching grind down Ratón Pass, I had almost convinced myself I'd experienced a psychotic break and imagined the monstrous creatures and the murders inside the Sangre de Cristo Mountains. But the word is "almost." I'll explain why.

I saw the train coming and began running with it, pacing my speed so I could throw my duffel and guitar inside an open car, when a yard bull grabbed me from behind and pulled me away from the tracks.

"I'll be out of the state in ten minutes, boss," I said. "How about some slack?"

"Sorry, bud," he replied. "It's your misfortune and none of my own."

"We're talking about six months on the hard road, boss."

"Life's a bitch, then we die," he said.

He walked me to the freight depot and called the cops. Guess who pulled in?

"How you doin', Wade?" I said.

"I hear you've been busy," he said.

"I got drunk and let my imagination run away."

"Where you going?"

"Down on the Cal-Mex line."

"Stay here a minute."

Wade walked out of earshot with the yard bull, then shook hands with him and rejoined me. "There's a highballer leaving out in ten minutes. I'll stay with you until you climb aboard. Want some coffee?"

"No, thank you."

He reached for his thermos through the driver's window of his car. "What happened in that box canyon?" he said.

"Nothing."

"Sure about that?"

"Sure as there are no witches except in Joseph McCarthy's sick mind."

"Need any money?"

"No, sir. It's been an honor to know you."

"Put me in one of your books."

"What's that in the back seat?" I asked.

He lit a Lucky Strike and exhaled the smoke through his nostrils. "A pilgrim hat." He reached in the window and put it on his head. "We're having a Little Theater rehearsal tonight. I play a Puritan judge."

"No kidding?" I said.

"Keep on the sunny side, kid. Don't look back. Something might be gaining on you."

"Satchel Paige said that."

"I knew you were smart."

In the early hours of the next day, somewhere in the Grand Canyon country around Flagstaff, the sliding door of my box-car open, I woke to the sweet smell of pines and the singing of the rails, just as the morning sun broke over the mountains and, in a blink, gave life to the shadows of the boxcars racing across the desert floor.

Acknowledgments

Once again I would like to thank my editor, Sean Manning, and Tzipora Baitch and Jackie Seow and the rest of the Simon & Schuster team for their help in the production of *Another Kind of Eden*. My thanks also to my copy editors, E. Beth Thomas and Jonathan Evans, and the Spitzer Agency, and thanks to my wife, Pearl, and our daughter Pamala, whom we lost recently.

I would also like to thank the readers of my work. They are more than just readers; they have become friends of the most loyal kind, sharing in our mutual desire to protect and save the earth and all its inhabitants.

Blessed be God for all dappled things.

James Lee Burke

About the Author

James Lee Burke is the author of many novels, and the critically-acclaimed, bestselling Detective Dave Robicheaux series. He won the Edgar Award for both *Cimarron Rose* and *Black Cherry Blues* and *Sunset Limited* was awarded the CWA Gold Dagger. *Two for Texas* was adapted for television, and *Heaven's Prisoners* and *In the Electric Mist* for film. Burke has been a Breadloaf Fellow and Guggenheim Fellow, has been awarded the Grand Master Award by the Mystery Writers of America and has been nominated for a Pulitzer award. He lives with his wife, Pearl, in Missoula, Montana.

www.JamesLeeBurke.com